LADY

AND THE
CONSPIRACY

A WALT WILLIAMS
MYSTERY/COMEDY NOVEL

ROBERT
THORNHILL

1

Lady Justice and the Conspiracy

Copyright July, 2015 by Robert Thornhill
All rights reserved.

This novel is a work of fiction. Names, incidents and entities included in the story are products of the author's imagination. Any resemblance to actual persons, events and entities is entirely coincidental.

Published in the United States of America

Cover design by Peg Thornhill
  1. Fiction, Humorous
  2. Fiction, Mystery & Detective, General

What People Are Saying About
The Lady Justice Mystery/Comedy Series

He takes what goes on in the world at the moment and incorporates it into his books. C. Toste – Amazon Review

Ripping scenes from recent headlines, Robert Thornhill has written one of his best novels yet. Sandy Penny – Amazon Review

Robert Thornhill walks a story teller's tightrope. Cynthia Butcher – Amazon Review

This author continually amazes me with how he can write a story about a current event without offensive finger pointing. He has a gift for writing both sides of the story. Heather – Amazon Review

As usual, Thornhill weaves an exciting, action packed story around social commentary of today's moral issues. His close proximity to the actual events, and his well-researched story line, produce a thought provoking novel. C.F. Jones – Amazon Review

This book really struck a nerve. Amazon Review

Way too real for fiction. B.A. Hawk – Amazon Review

A fascinating controversial story. Sheri Wilkinson – Amazon Review

Thornhill always takes current relevant topics and writes great stories around them. Nancy Williams – Amazon Review

The Lady Justice series takes a hard look at some of the moral dilemmas of our Times. K9sage – Amazon Review

Treats controversial subject with delicacy and without judgment. Leaves readers food for thought. Readers able to draw own conclusion. Jean Butala – Amazon Review

Thornhill has brilliantly used a fictional comedic mystery story to force us to remove the blinders and take a peek at reality. Mr. Thornhill has an uncanny talent for bringing our attention to a serious problem while also entertaining and amusing us. Lee Ashford- Taken from a review on Readers' Favorite

This is yet another gripping novel by Thornhill, who spins the web so intricately the reader is unable to take a break before completing the book. Venky – Amazon Review

LADY JUSTICE AND THE CONSPIRACY

CHAPTER 1

Jack Carson switched on the dome light of his car and looked at his watch for the fourth time. The man he was supposed to meet was forty-five minutes late.

His first contact with the man who would only identify himself as 'Falcon' was two weeks ago. He had told Carson he had contacted him because he had seen his name in numerous bylines in the *Kansas City Star*. It certainly made sense. Carson was the number one guy working the *Star's* crime beat. His name was connected to at least a half-dozen stories every day; everything from drive-by shootings to domestic disturbances.

Carson had nearly hung up on the guy when Falcon announced he was an Air Force pilot who had been recruited to fly missions solely for the purpose of dispersing deadly chemicals into the atmosphere. Carson received bogus calls every day which included everything from Elvis sightings to alien spacecraft landings, and part of his job was to sort the newsworthy tips from the obviously absurd.

He was about to dismiss the guy as just another crackpot when he happened to glance out the window and see a series of fluffy white trails crisscrossing the sky. The trails had become so commonplace he hardly paid any attention to them anymore, but he remembered wondering once, why there seemed to be so many more and why they lasted so long before dispersing and forming a grey haze which blocked the rays of the sun.

What the hell, he had thought. It was a slow news day and what did he have to lose other than an hour of time? He agreed to meet the man for the first of what turned into three clandestine meetings; all were at secluded locations and all were under the cover of darkness.

The first time they met, Carson had halfway expected to see a guy wearing one of those tin foil hats which are supposed to keep evil forces from reading your thoughts, but quite the contrary, the man could have been the poster boy from an Air Force recruiting ad. He could have been Tom Cruise's stand-in as Maverick in the movie, *Top Gun*.

Falcon made it clear from the beginning he was to remain anonymous and under no circumstances could the information he would give be attributed to him. If his identity was disclosed, at the very least he would be court martialed --- or worse.

Just like Woodward and Bernstein's 'Deep Throat' in All the President's Men, Carson thought as he listened to Falcon's demand for anonymity.

At that meeting, and the two which followed, Falcon shared details which turned Carson's blood cold. He took meticulous notes about the men who were recruited to fly the covert missions, the planes that were loaded with deadly chemicals and the purpose of the 'chemtrails' which stretched from horizon to horizon across the entire United States.

After each meeting, Carson would spend long hours trying to verify what Falcon had given him. He found enough evidence to give some credibility to the frightful scenario which Falcon had painted --- enough that he was willing to move forward if Falcon could provide him with the one piece of evidence which would convince him the story was true --- a sample of the brew Falcon said was pumped into barrels in the huge bellies of the Boeing KC-135 Stratotankers. Falcon had agreed and was supposed to deliver the sample at tonight's meeting.

Carson looked at his watch again. Falcon was an hour late and probably not coming. His story had been captivating, but when pressured to produce the one thing which could verify his wild claims, he would come up empty, because his story was just that --- wild claims which could not be substantiated.

Carson sighed, started the car and headed home. On the one hand, he was relieved. It would be far better for our country if Falcon's assertions were figments of his imagination. On the other hand, if what Falcon shared was true, the story he would have written had Pulitzer Prize written all over it.

The next morning, Carson was at his desk reviewing the stories from the night before. There was nothing earth-shattering, but one piece about a fatal car wreck caught his eye. The accident had taken place just a mile from where he was to meet Falcon. He vaguely remembered hearing sirens as he waited for the whistle-blower to make his appearance.

Naturally, the name associated with the story meant nothing to him. He had only known the informant as Falcon.

Finally, his curiosity got the most of him and he headed to the county morgue.

His position on the paper's crime beat had taken him to the morgue many times and he knew the people running the place by name. All he had to do was ask and the attendant led him to the vault where the body from the previous night's wreck was stored.

A cold chill ran through his body when the attendant pulled out what was left of the man who was supposed to bring him evidence of a massive covert plan which, if true, was affecting every citizen in the United States. The attendant identified him as Dale Fox, a pilot in the US Air Force.

He thanked the attendant and as he headed to his car, he pulled out his cell phone and scrolled through the names until he found the name of the officer who had filed the report, George Wilson.

Nearly everyone called the officer Ox, because of his robust size. Carson placed the call and a sleepy voice answered, "What do you want Carson? I worked last night and I'm trying to get some shut-eye."

"Ahh, caller ID. The age of technology. Actually, that's why I'm calling. You made a report on a car wreck with a fatality last night. I have a few questions."

"If you read the report, there's not much more I can tell you. It was pretty cut and dried. It looked like the guy lost control on a curve and rolled into a tree. Probably died on impact."

"So you didn't find anything out of the ordinary?"

"Like what?"

"I don't know. Just something which didn't look right."

"Nope, nothing like that."

"One more thing and I'll let you go. Did you happen to find a vial of some kind of liquid in the car?"

"No, again. What kind of liquid? You mean like booze? There was no alcohol in the car."

"Okay, thanks for your time. Sorry I woke you."

As Carson pulled out into traffic, he remembered Falcon talking about his commanding officer's dire predictions of what might happen to any pilot divulging information about the program known among the aviators and crews as 'Indigo Skyfold.'

Falcon had done just that, and now he was dead.

A coincidence?

Carson didn't think so.

CHAPTER 2

Surveillance is boring and mind-numbing and I had been doing it for three solid hours.

Actually, I should have been grateful for the boredom. During my five years as a Kansas City police officer, I had been shot, beaten, thrown off a roof and nearly blown up so many times, I finally made the decision to turn in my badge and at the ripe old age of seventy-two, open my own private investigation company. I figured I could choose the cases I wanted to work and avoid any which put life and limb in jeopardy.

Unfortunately, that had not been the case. In the few short months Walt Williams Investigations had been in business, I had tangled with the Russian mob, a serial killer, and terrorists with ties to Al-Qaeda.

Three of my previous cases had involved tailing a subject and taking a few photos from the safety of my car, all of which paid handsomely and totally avoided personal injury to my aging body. I figured my current gig would fall into that category.

I had been hired by a woman who suspected her husband was fooling around. My job was to tail the guy and catch him in the act. I had followed him to a motel on Broadway and got a shot of him entering one of the rooms. To my dismay, his lady friend didn't step outside so I resigned myself to sitting in the parking lot hoping to get her on film when their tryst was over.

I figured if he was like most men, he would take care of business and be out in twenty minutes tops, but the guy must have had exceptional stamina and the clock had ticked off three hours.

Otto Kruger was certainly a healthy specimen. He was a nose tackle for a semi-pro team and had to be at least 6'6" and weigh 320 pounds. He was used to pounding an offensive line for sixty grueling minutes, so maybe three hours in the sack wasn't such a stretch.

I had come prepared with all the accoutrements of a P.I. on surveillance. In addition to my binoculars and digital camera, I had a full thermos of coffee and a bag of snacks. I would have preferred a box of Krispy Kreme donuts, but my sweet and protective wife, Maggie, had nixed that idea and provided me with protein bars and a bag of trail mix.

As I sat there, listening to my Elvis CD's and munching on the nuts and seeds which came in my trail mix, I thought about Euell Gibbons, the old guy on the Grape Nuts cereal commercials and wondered what ever happened to him. Strange how your mind wanders when your butt's been glued to a car seat for 180 minutes.

I had just poured the last of my coffee when the motel door opened. Kruger came out, paused, and turned for a good-bye kiss from his illicit lover.

She was visible just long enough for me to snap her picture.

Job well done.

I was feeling quite elated until Kruger turned and saw me checking the shot on my camera screen. Our eyes locked for just a moment, and my elation turned to concern and then to sheer terror as the behemoth charged toward my car.

I quickly checked to make sure my doors were locked and reached for my keys which had been in the ignition powering my accessories during my vigil. I figured that discretion being the better part of valor, my best bet was to make a hasty exit. I had what I needed and there was absolutely nothing to be gained by hanging around.

Imagine my disappointment when I turned the switch and all I got was a low growl. Three hours of Elvis tunes had sucked the life out of my battery. Kruger was charging hard and I was dead in the water.

I thought about escaping on foot, but there just wasn't time.

As he approached, his face was flaming red, eyes bulging and jaw set. It was then I remembered his wife telling me he had been cut from the Oakland Raiders for anger management issues.

His fist was as big as a Honey Baked Ham and the moment he reached the car, he slammed it into my hood, leaving a cantaloupe-sized dent.

"The camera!" he shouted. "Give it to me. Now!"

I didn't respond. I just sat there in shock trying to figure a way out of the mess.

He pounded the roof. "Give me that damned camera or I'll rip off your head and shit down your neck!"

I recognized the line from Stanley Kubrick's 1987 war movie, *Full Metal Jacket*, and I briefly wondered if Otto was a film buff or if his act was just something that came naturally to him. Either way, it didn't really matter. He had made his point.

As he beat on my roof, I regretted I had left my gun at home. I have a concealed carry permit, but I never dreamed I should be packing heat on a lame surveillance gig. Live and learn.

When the pounding didn't produce the desired result, Kruger adopted a different tactic. He began rocking the car back and forth. The specter of this huge man moving two tons of steel brought to mind Lou Ferrigno as the *Incredible Hulk*.

I hung onto the steering wheel for dear life while coffee splashed and trail mix scattered. When this was all over, I would have a nasty mess to clean up, assuming, of course, that I would survive.

After one final shove, he glared at me through the window. "Hand it over or I'm coming in to get it!"

When I didn't respond, he stormed off, searching the parking lot for something to bash in my window. It didn't take a genius to know once he was inside, I was toast.

I reached for my cell phone and punched the speed dial for my former partner, Ox.

"Hey, Walt! What's up?"

"Where are you? I hope to heck you're close by."

"Main and Linwood. What's going on? You sound terrible."

"Get over here as fast as you can. I'm in the parking lot of the motel at Linwood and Broadway. A 300 pound Neanderthal is about to rip off my head!"

"On my way. You can explain when I get there."

I heard the siren in the distance and I just hoped Ox would get here in time to save my ass. Kruger had just wrestled a handicapped parking sign out of the asphalt parking lot and was heading my way.

He had just aimed the sign post at my driver's window when Ox roared into the parking lot. I ducked for cover and heard his booming voice on the loud speaker.

"Drop the sign! Do it now!"

The sight of Ox and his new partner, Amanda Parrish, bailing out of their cruiser with guns drawn evidently got Kruger's attention. He didn't hit the car, but he didn't drop the pole either.

15

As Ox and Amanda advanced, I saw Kruger scowl, raise the six foot sign over his head and fling it at my friends. They both ducked, but the metal pole struck Ox in the head and knocked the gun out of Amanda's hand.

Seeing they were both temporarily distracted, Kruger charged at Amanda, ignoring Ox who was on the ground, dazed. Amanda deftly side-stepped the huge nose tackle's charge and as he stumbled past, turned and planted her foot squarely between his legs.

The big man stopped in his tracks and I could see his body quiver as the blow to his gonads resonated through his body. He staggered a few steps and crumpled, face down, into the asphalt. Amanda was on him in a flash and cuffed his hands behind his back.

It occurred to me that like Euell Gibbons, Otto Kruger would probably have grape nuts the next morning.

As soon as he was down, I rushed to Ox's side. He had a nasty cut on his head, but seemed to be okay otherwise.

He looked at the beached whale lying beside him in handcuffs. "Unbelievable! I thought you were only taking cream puff cases. I guess not."

"It was supposed to be," I replied. "Thanks --- again. The two of you pulled my fat out of the fire."

I shared my side of the story as we waited for the paddy wagon to arrive and haul Kruger to lock-up.

After Otto, still reeling from Amanda's well-placed punt, was loaded, I got a jump start from the meat wagon before it headed back to the precinct.

I stopped at the Soapy Suds car wash and vacuumed the trail mix from the front seat.

As I headed home, I marveled that once again, Lady Justice had prevailed, the bad guy was in jail and I had avoided another encounter with the grim reaper by the skin of my teeth.

I was about to call my client and tell her I had the goods on her cheating husband, when the phone rang.

"Hi Walt. This is Jack Carson."

I knew Carson very well. He was the top crime reporter for the *Kansas City Star*. He must have a police scanner because he was johnny-on-the-spot at most every crime scene Ox and I worked. Inevitably, he would press us for information about what was going on, and without exception, I would always reply, "No comment."

I knew the guy was just doing his job, but the last thing I wanted was to be the source he quoted in the next day's paper.

I figured he had gotten wind of my encounter with Otto Kruger and was fishing for a story.

"Look, Jack, I'm not a cop anymore. If you want information on a case, call the precinct."

"That's not what this is about. I'd like to come by and talk to you."

I was still in my clothes which were wet and stained from the coffee that was sloshing around while Otto was rocking my car. "It's not a good time. Can't we just talk on the phone?"

He hesitated. "I'd rather not. What I want to discuss is rather sensitive and you never know who might be listening."

His comment aroused my curiosity. "Give me a half hour."

Thirty minutes later, Carson was sitting in my office.

"I know what I'm about to tell you will sound crazy, but please hear me out."

For the next hour, Carson told me how Dale Fox, whom he knew only as Falcon, had come to him with the incredible story of being a pilot in a clandestine, black ops program whose mission was to alter and control the world's weather by spraying chemtrails of deadly poisons into the atmosphere. He gave me details of their three meetings, and ended by sharing what he knew of

18

the accident which had prevented Falcon from delivering the evidence which would verify his claims.

When he finished, I sat in stunned disbelief.

"Why are you telling me all of this? What can I do?"

"The reason I've come to you is the officer who covered the wreck was your old partner, Ox. You must know if I went to the cops with this story, they'd laugh me out of the precinct and my credibility would be gone forever. All I'm asking you to do is talk to Ox and ask him to take a closer look at the accident scene. On the surface, it appeared to be just another traffic mishap, but knowing the background of the situation, wouldn't you agree his untimely death just as he was about to blow the whistle on a covert government scheme is quite a coincidence?"

I had to agree that it was.

"I'll talk to Ox, but I can't promise anything."

"That's all I ask."

I gave Ox a call, but he was at the hospital getting his wound dressed.

I finally reached him an hour later.

"Hey, Partner, how's the head?"

"I've got a killer headache and five stitches. This thing is gonna leave a scar."

"I'm sure it will only enhance the vision of your rugged manhood."

"Thanks a lot."

"I need a favor."

"Another one! I just saved your ass. How many do you want in one day?"

"Just one more, I promise."

"Well, as long as it doesn't involve a 300 pound gorilla coming at me with a traffic sign, I might consider it."

"You worked a case the other night, a Dale Fox wrapped his car around a tree."

"You're the second person who's called me about that case. The crime reporter, Jack Carson, called too. What's going on?"

"It's a long story. What I'd like you to do is have the crime scene guys take another look at the car, particularly the brake line. Remember the young couple who bought a house from Maggie and ran into the back of a semi on the way to sign the contract?"

"Yeah, I remember. Their brake line had been cut just enough to cause it to rupture. Do you believe something like that is going on here?"

"It's certainly a possibility. What about family? Have you notified his next of kin?"

"Dead end. His parents are deceased, he had no siblings and he was never married. The guy was all alone."

That certainly lined up with what Falcon had told Carson. He said the pilots were chosen from the top ranks of the Air Force, Navy and Coast Guard. One of the qualifiers was lack of familial connections. They wanted men who were 'hardened' and had no qualms about spraying toxic substances into the atmosphere. He actually referred to them as 'Tanker Terminators.'

"Even more reason to take a second look. Will you do it?"

"I will. I just hope you're not getting me mixed up in another of your crazy cases."

I didn't have the heart to tell him I just might be doing that very thing.

Later that day, Ox called back.

"You were right on, Partner. The brake line had ruptured, causing him to lose control on the curve. The bad news is there is not sufficient evidence to support the idea the line was deliberately cut. It could have just been worn and ruptured on its own."

"Well, we both know someone with skills can cut the line just enough for the thing to rupture when pressure is applied."

"True enough, but in this situation, there is nothing to suggest that happened, so the case is closed. Sorry."

"Thanks, I appreciate you looking into it."

"Glad to help."

Just as he was hanging up, I had another thought. "One more thing. Did you get an address on the guy and has anyone from the department gone by his place?"

He thought for a moment. "Yeah, I got an address, but no one's been there. Once it was determined it was an accident, there was no reason for us to pursue the matter further. You want the address?"

"Yes, please." As he was looking it up, I recalled my days as a landlord. More than once a tenant had died or disappeared and I didn't know about it until the rent was late and I came knocking for payment.

Ox came back on the line. "Got it. An apartment on Brookside, south of the Plaza. I'm guessing you're going there."

"Probably will. I need to tie up a few loose ends."

As far as the cops were concerned the case might be closed, but for me, it was just beginning.

CHAPTER 3

The moment I hung up from Ox, I dialed Kevin McBride, my brother-in-law and partner in Walt Williams Investigations.

"Hey Walt! How'd it go with Otto Kruger? Was he playing 'hide the salami' with some chick like his wife suspected?"

"Indeed he was and I got it all on camera, but that's not why I'm calling. Can you come over? We need to talk."

"Geese Walt, Victoria will be home any time now and I was thinking about hiding some salami myself. Why can't we just talk on the phone?"

I had already considered that possibility, but then I remembered Jack Carson saying, "You never know who might be listening." If Dale Fox was about to expose a government conspiracy, it wasn't a stretch to believe Big Brother was listening to anyone and everyone even remotely connected to the case.

"Come on, Kevin. This is important. You can dip your wick tonight."

"Okay, okay! Give me a half hour."

Thirty minutes later, Kevin was in my office listening to what I knew about the chemtrail conspiracy.

He listened quietly and when I finished he just shook his head. "It was bound to happen sooner or later."

"What was bound to happen?"

"One of those pilots would have an attack of conscience and the balls to tell the world we're being poisoned by our government."

I was in shock. "So you believe in this conspiracy thing?"

"I believe chemicals are being sprayed into the air. For Chris' sakes, Walt. All you have to do is look up most any day of the week and see dozens of fluffy trails crisscrossing the sky. The official word is those are water condensation trails, but that's bureaucratic bullshit. We have them almost every day here in Kansas City, but it was much worse in Phoenix."

Before coming to Kansas City, Kevin lived in Phoenix for thirty years and worked as a private investigator.

"Angel hair," he continued. "That's what we would call the stuff which fell on us after the sky had been obliterated by the chemical emissions. They looked like very long cobwebs, but unlike cobwebs they would completely dissolve into our skin when we touched them. When we held a match to them, they would blacken and curl like plastic or some polymer burning. Scary stuff!"

I was stunned by what my partner was saying. "If that's true and the stuff was falling everywhere, why didn't someone report it?

"Oh, they did!" he replied. "The Air Force denied they were spraying chemicals and the EPA said there was nothing to worry about. So who you gonna call next? Ghostbusters?"

"Unbelievable!"

"No kidding. If it's the government doing the dirty work, it's not going to do much good to go to them for help."

"Back to our present situation. If Dale Fox was telling the truth, there just might be some evidence in his apartment. The cops think his death was an accident and didn't even take a look. Are you interested?"

"You bet I am!" he replied with a grin.

"Got your lock picks?"

"Does Howdy Doody have wooden balls?"

Dale Fox's apartment was on the second floor of a brick four-plex on Brookside.

It took Kevin less than a minute to pop the deadbolt and get us inside. The place was a typical bachelor pad, small living area with a TV, an eat-in kitchen, bedroom and bath.

Falcon's kitchen looked a lot like my own before Maggie and I were married. There was a carton of milk which expired two weeks ago and a loaf of bread with green stuff around the edges in the fridge. A can of Spicy Hot Spam, a can of chicken noodle soup, and a box of saltines were on the shelf beside the stove. Typical fare for a single guy who spent most of his time flying jets across the country.

We found nothing of interest until we opened the drawer of the nightstand beside his bed.

"Bingo!" Kevin exclaimed as he pulled two photos out of the drawer.

I looked over his shoulder. The first photo was of airplanes with no visible names or lettering. On the back were the words 'Pinal Air Park, Arizona.'

The second photo showed the interior of a huge jet which seemed to be filled with canisters of some kind.

"This must be some of the evidence Fox was going to give to Jack Carson," I said, taking a closer look.

"So what do we do with it?" Kevin asked.

I thought for a moment. "We can't just take it. We're not even supposed to be here and if we did take it, we could never prove where we got it. Let's leave it here. I'll call Ox and tell him what we've found. He can say he received an anonymous tip that there was incriminating evidence in Fox's apartment, then when they search and find it, it can be used as evidence --- if this conspiracy thing ever goes anywhere, and that's a big 'if.'"

"Sounds good to me," he said, tucking the photos back where we'd found them.

I called Ox and made arrangements to meet him in the precinct parking lot after his shift. For the second time that day, I didn't want to chance a phone conversation which might be overheard.

"What's up?" he asked, sliding into the seat beside me.

I told him the story and what we had found.

Like me, he was stunned. "Holy Crap, Walt! You're telling me the government is filling the skies with poison and this Fox guy was one of the pilots and was going to blow the whistle. Then you're saying he got whacked before he could verify his story and the proof is in the nightstand by his bed!"

"That's it in a nutshell."

"Do you know how utterly ridiculous that sounds?"

"Of course I do, but don't you think it would be worth your time to get those photos and establish a chain of custody just in case it isn't?"

He shook his head. "How in heaven's name do you get mixed up in all this weird stuff?"

"Just lucky I guess. Will you do it?"

He sighed. "Yeah, I'll do it, but I think you're way out in left field on this one."

At ten the next morning, my phone rang.

"Walt, it's Ox. We went to Fox's apartment and went over the place with a fine toothed comb and guess what --- no photos! Nothing but some stale milk and bread. Are you sure you and Kevin aren't smoking something?"

"But --- they were there yesterday!"

"Well, they're not there today. Sorry, Pal."

"Someone must have been there after we were. Probably the same people who sabotaged Fox's car. You can see that, can't you?"

"What I see is a crazy theory and no proof to back it up. I really am sorry, Walt. Well, I've got to concoct some story as to why I wasted the department's time. Talk to you later."

The missing photos were just one more bit of evidence Jack Carson was on to something. I was really pissed they had disappeared.

It was a good thing I had photographed them with my phone.

CHAPTER 4

I had just hung up from Ox when the phone jingled again.

"Walt, Jack Carson here. Sorry to bother you but I was just wondering if you persuaded Ox to take another look at Fox's accident."

So much had happened so fast I had totally forgotten to keep Carson in the loop. Since he was the one who opened this can of worms, I figured I should bring him up to date.

"Actually, I've got a lot to share with you, but I don't think we should discuss it on the phone."

"I agree. I know you like Mel's Diner. How about we meet there and I'll buy you a piece of pie?"

Carson had certainly done his homework. Mel's was indeed my favorite greasy spoon. "Sounds good to me. I can be there in fifteen minutes."

"So you're telling me the accident was caused by a ruptured brake line, but there's not enough evidence to confirm it was tampered with?" Carson asked, shoveling a huge bite of coconut cream pie into his mouth.

"That's what the CSI guys are saying, so as far as the cops are concerned, case closed."

"Quite a coincidence don't you think, that a brake line would rupture on the very night Fox was bringing me evidence of a conspiracy?"

"That's exactly what I thought, so that's why my partner, Kevin McBride, and I took a look inside Fox's apartment."

"You did? How in the world did you get keys and permission?"

"Do you really need to know that?" I asked with a grimace.

"Never mind," he replied with a knowing nod. "So did you find anything?"

"Sure did," I replied, pulling out my cell phone. "We found these photos in the drawer of his nightstand."

"Son-of-a bitch!" he exclaimed, examining the photos. "The unmarked planes and the canisters inside which hold the chemicals. It's just like he described them to me. So where are the actual photos?"

I sighed. "That's another story. We left them where we found them and I persuaded Ox to get a team together to go through Fox's apartment. We wanted them to be found by the cops to establish a chain of custody."

"That's real smart," Carson said. "So the cops have the photos now?"

I shook my head. "Ox's team went through the entire apartment and didn't find a thing. Now, unfortunately, both he and I look like fools."

"Damn!" Carson muttered slamming his fist on the table. "They cleaned the place out after you left and before the cops arrived."

"So it would seem, but who is 'they'?"

"That's the question, isn't it? This all fits with what Fox shared with me. Apparently he and a number of other pilots have questioned their superiors about what they had been ordered to spray. They were told in no uncertain terms to keep their mouths shut and do their jobs --- that it was a matter of national security. He even went on to say the planes were equipped with a cyber program called Flash Point or FP-03. He said the program was a self-destruct sequence that could be remotely activated from any ground, water surface, under water base or mobile air unit. He said the signal is encrypted through three satellites and cannot be blocked or jammed. They were told FP-03 exists so damaged planes could be detonated over safe zones instead of going down in populated areas, but the pilots were pretty sure this was a fail-safe program to prevent pilots from turning over incriminating evidence to any public, private or civilian authorities."

"I can imagine that would be pretty effective, knowing at any moment, 'they' could blow you and your plane to smithereens."

"Exactly! And if they're willing to blow up a plane rather than to have its clandestine mission revealed, I'm sure they wouldn't think twice about whacking a pilot who was about to spill the beans."

"So what now?" I asked. "We have no real evidence of any kind. Everything Falcon told you is hearsay. If you try to go public with what we have now, you'll just be written off as another nut case."

"Sadly, you are exactly right, but I'll tell you this, I'm not going to give up. I'm going to keep digging. Dale Fox was brutally murdered for trying to expose the truth and I'm not going to let that brave man die in vain."

On the way home, I kept thinking about the photo of the canisters inside the belly of the huge plane and wondered what kind of chemical was being spewed into our beautiful blue skies every day.

Then I remembered going out onto my front step one afternoon. My tenant, Leopold Skinner, or the Professor as he likes to be called, was gazing into the air.

"Beautiful day," I remarked.

He pointed to the white trails streaking the sky. "It was," he replied, "until the government intervened."

He went on to talk about the toxins which were polluting our air, but I was preoccupied with other things, and like most Americans, I had seen the trails in the sky for years. Besides, who in their right mind would even consider the possibility our very own government, sworn to protect its citizens, would do something so despicable.

Being a retired professor with doctorates in Psychology, Sociology and Philosophy, I figured he might be able to shed some light on the mysterious streaks in the sky, so I parked my car and headed to his apartment on the first floor of my building.

"Walt! Come in please. What brings you to my door this fine day?"

I pointed up. "Tell me what you know about the streaks across the sky."

He smiled. "What was it --- a year ago, maybe two --- I pointed those out to you but you just weren't interested. What's changed?"

I plopped into one of his easy chairs and told him everything which had happened since the first call from Jack Carson.

"So, I guess at this point I'd like to know what's being sprayed, who's doing the spraying and why are they doing it."

"My, my, you are an inquisitive lad. What makes you think I have the knowledge you're seeking?"

"Well, for one, you're the smartest person I know and I figured you would have the information or tell me where I could get it."

He rubbed his chin. "Very well, let's see what your attempt at flattery will get you. In a nutshell, the answer to your 'why' is weather control and national defense. Are you, by any chance, familiar with a paper titled, *Weather as a force multiplier. Controlling the weather in 2025*?"

I shook my head.

"I thought not. It was a paper published by the Air Force in 1996. It laid the groundwork for what we are seeing today. Hang on a minute."

He went to a bookcase and ran his fingers across a row of titles.

"Ahh, here it is."

He returned and opened the book to a dog-eared page.

"Let me just read some of the things being proposed back in 1996. *'In 2025, US aerospace forces can "own the weather" by capitalizing on emerging technologies and focusing development of those technologies to war-fighting applications. Such a capability offers the warfighter tools to shape the battlespace in ways never before possible. It provides opportunities to impact operations across the full spectrum of conflict and is pertinent to all possible futures. The purpose of this paper is to outline a strategy for the use of a future weather-modification system to achieve military objectives rather than to provide a detailed technical road map.'"*

He ran his finger down the page. "Here we go. *'Weather-modification technologies might involve techniques that would increase latent heat release in the atmosphere, provide additional water vapor for cloud cell development, and provide additional surface and lower atmospheric heating to increase atmospheric instability. Critical to the success of any attempt to trigger a storm cell is the pre-existing atmospheric conditions locally and regionally. The atmosphere must already be conditionally unstable and the large-scale dynamics must be supportive of vertical cloud development. The focus of the weather-modification effort would be to provide additional "conditions" that would make the atmosphere unstable enough to generate cloud and eventually storm cell development. The path of storm cells once developed or enhanced is dependent not only on the mesoscale dynamics of the storm but the regional and synoptic (global) scale atmospheric wind flow patterns in the area which are currently not subject to human control.'"*

He continued to scan the page. "Ahh yes, and here's how they plan to do it. *'A number of methods have been explored or proposed to modify the ionosphere, including injection of chemical vapors and heating or charging via electromagnetic radiation or particle beams (such as ions, neutral particles, x-rays, MeV particles, and energetic electrons). It is important to note that many techniques to modify the upper atmosphere have been successfully demonstrated experimentally.'"*

"Any of that sound familiar?" he asked.

"I heard 'injection of chemical vapors,' and I'm guessing those are the streaks across the sky, but the rest of it doesn't mean a thing to me."

"You are quite right about the vapors, but those chemicals are only half of the equation. Have you ever heard of HAARP?"

Of course, I had not.

He thumbed through the book again. "HAARP is a research station in Gakona, Alaska. It is funded by the Air Force, the Navy, the University of Alaska and DARPA, the Defense Advanced Projects Agency. Let me read a description of the facility to you. *'It's the largest ionospheric heater in the world. Capable of heating a 1000 square kilometer area of the ionosphere to over 50,000 degrees. It's also a phased array. Which means it's steer-able and those waves can be directed to a selected target area. What they have found is that by sending radio frequency energy up and focusing it, as they do with these kinds of instruments, it causes a heating effect. And that heating literally lifts the ionosphere within a 30 mile diameter area therein changing localized pressure systems or perhaps the route of jet streams. Moving a jet stream is a phenomenal event in terms of man being able to do this. The problem is we cannot model the system adequately. Long term consequences of atmospheric heating are unknown. Changing weather in one place can have a devastating downstream effect. And HAARP has already been accused of modifying the weather.'"*

"Here's a photo of it," he said, handing me the book.

"So you think the government is altering the weather with this thing?"

"It would certainly seem so, and with disastrous results, I might add."

He reached into a newspaper rack beside his chair. *"The Kansas City Star*, Sunday, May31st, 2015," he said opening the paper. "The headline reads *Worldwide, the weather is weird.* It talks about the drought in California, the floods in Texas, the 91 degree heat in Alaska, and the record snowfall in Boston. They talk about global warming and El Nino, but the real culprits are the blasts from HAARP which heat a 1000 square kilometer area of the ionosphere to over 50,000 degrees. The jet stream controls our weather, that's an undisputable fact, and the jet stream is undoubtedly altered by HAARP. Storms that would have normally dropped rain on the west coast have been diverted north, over the Arctic Circle and down onto the east coast."

"Okay, I think I understand about the weather aspect, but what about the military part. Why are the Navy and Air Force so invested in these projects?"

"A very good question and one which is out of my area of expertise. If you want to know more about the military's involvement, let me refer you to a colleague of mine at the university, Dr. Frank Katz. He's done extensive research on the subject."

I thanked the Professor and as I headed out the door, I paused. "Tell me, Professor, if all of this is going on, why aren't more people up in arms about it?"

He shrugged. "Apathy, the curse of modern society. Why do only fifty percent of the voting population cast their votes in the presidential election? Frustration, as in, you can't fight city hall. The government is just too big and powerful. Complacency, as in, I'm doing all right, why rock the boat. As I recall, the last time we discussed this subject, you didn't give a damn either."

He was right. I didn't give a damn then, but I certainly did now.

CHAPTER 5

I left the Professor's apartment and was heading to my own on the third floor when I met Jerry on the second floor landing.

"Hey Walt, do you know what you get when you cross a chicken and a ghost?"

Jerry fancied himself to be the second coming of Rodney Dangerfield and was constantly trying out new material for his weekly act on amateur night at the local comedy club.

I just wasn't in the mood for levity, so I snapped back, "Not today, Jerry!"

I saw the crestfallen look on his face and realized I was being an ass. "Sorry, I just have a lot on my mind. Please tell me what you get when you cross a chicken and a ghost."

He brightened immediately. "A poultry-geist, of course. So what's got you all bent out of shape?"

I wasn't about to go into detail regarding the conspiracy theory with a stand-up comic, so I simply said, "The Professor and I were discussing the jet trails across the sky."

"Beautiful, aren't they?" he said wistfully. "Did you see the ones last night right at sunset? They looked like a big Tic-Tac-Toe game in the sky. Then they turned all pink and gold from the rays of the setting sun. It was just gorgeous."

"I'm sure it was," I replied, climbing the last flight of stairs.

So there it was. The reaction of the average man on the street, totally awed by the phenomenon and totally unaware the brilliant colors were being reflected from poisons sprayed into the sky. One more example of wolves disguised in sheep's clothing.

The Professor had used that analogy one other time when describing the wonders of modern technology like cell phones, computers and On Star, which on the surface make our lives so much easier but which also open portals into our private lives so Big Brother can keep tabs on us. I really didn't believe him until it was revealed the NSA was monitoring our phone conversations and email.

Wolves in sheep's clothing.

That's what was on my mind when I opened the door to my apartment.

Maggie must have heard me chatting in the hall. She greeted me with a big hug and a smooch.

"I see you made it through the Jerry gauntlet."

"Yes, but not unscathed. Poultry-geist."

"Yeah, I got that too when I went for the mail. You seem tense. What's bothering you?"

Maggie can read me like a book. We had only been married six years, but I learned early on I might as well come clean with her because somehow, she gets to the bottom of everything that's going on in my life.

"It's a long story."

"Well, I've got all night. How about I get you a glass of Arbor Mist and you can tell me all about it?"

It actually took two glasses of Arbor Mist to get through the entire tale of the alleged government conspiracy. When I finished, I could see the concern on her face and I knew what was coming.

During my five years on the police force, I had placed not only myself, but my family and friends in harm's way. It took a bullet in my buttocks to make me realize I had escaped the clutches of the grim reaper one too many times. That's when I made the decision to turn in my badge and open my own detective agency where I could choose cases which wouldn't put myself and my loved ones in peril.

"Walt, if what you're saying is true and this Falcon was silenced to prevent him from talking, it sounds like these people, whoever they are, wouldn't hesitate to take out anyone threatening to reveal their secrets."

I nodded. "You're probably right."

"So then, exactly what are you planning to do? I hope you're not going to get mixed up in this thing."

"No, of course not. I'm smart enough to know challenging the government is like Don Quixote tilting at windmills. The last thing I want is to put you and my friends in danger, but ---."

"But what?" she asked, and I saw the look I always get when I'm about to do something stupid.

"I'm not going to get involved, but I'm certain Jack Carson is. All I'm going to do is feed him as much background information as I can find and then I'm done --- out of it completely, and he can do what he wants with it. As a reporter for a major newspaper, he is certainly in a better position to get the truth out to the public."

I could see she was skeptical. "Somehow you're going to get sucked into this thing. I just know it."

"I won't. I promise."

The next morning, I parked my car on Cherry Street and walked the few blocks to the University of Missouri-Kansas City campus. After asking a few passing students, I was directed to the teacher's lounge in the Arts and Sciences building.

Seated at one of the tables was an elderly gentleman with a full beard who reminded me of the stand-up comedian, Foster Brooks.

He waved me over. "Frank Katz," he said, extending his hand. "You must be Walt Williams. My old friend, Professor Skinner, told me you'd be dropping by. How can I help you?"

"Well, this may sound a bit off the wall, but I'd like to know what you know about the chemtrails.

The Professor said you were somewhat of an expert on the military aspects of the trails."

"I don't know if 'expert' is the correct term," he said with a twinkle in his eye, "but I have done a bit of research on the subject. Ever heard of Project Cloverleaf?"

I shook my head.

"I'm not surprised. Very few have, and yet it's one of our most sophisticated defense systems. Cloverleaf involves a combination of chemtrails for creating an atmosphere which will support electromagnetic waves, ground-based electromagnetic field oscillators called gyrotrons and ionospheric heaters."

"The Professor told me about the ionospheric heater. I think it's called HAARP."

"Very good! Here's how it works. They spray barium powders and let them photo-ionize from the ulataviolet light of the sun. Then, they make an aluminum-plasma generated by 'zapping' the metal cations which are in the spray with either electromagnetics from HAARP, the gyrotron system on the ground called GWEN, or space-based lasers. The barium makes the aluminum plasma more particulate dense."

"Ummm, I don't want to appear stupid, but what's a cation?"

"That's certainly not a stupid question. Cations are atoms which have lost an electron to become positively charged. In short, chemtrails are the medium and directed energy is the method. Spray and zap!"

"But why? What are they trying to accomplish?"

"It all goes back to the Cold War with Russia. Surely you remember the days when the Soviet Union was stockpiling intercontinental ballistic missiles and aiming them at the United States."

"I certainly do. People were building underground bomb shelters and socking away food and water in case of a nuclear attack. It was a scary time."

"Indeed it was, and that's why this technology was invented. By deploying the HAARP system, no missiles from Russia would reach the US. None. Zero. And that was pretty effective! Most people think of an ICBM as a kind of big rock or arrow. You just lob it from here and it sorta lands on the target over there. Not so. An ICBM is a space vehicle. It must take off using a large booster rocket, travel at near orbital speed in the vacuum of space until it is over the target, then it must re-enter the atmosphere.

"To survive re-entry the missile must use one of several schemes, like retro rockets, or deploying an ablative heat shield to protect the warhead from simply burning up in the atmosphere. If the missile's computer controls are destroyed when passing through the magnetosphere then the missile will not survive re-entry and will simply burn up like a piece of space junk or a meteor.

There's a good chance the missile's control systems are destroyed even before the second stage separates from the booster, thus the missile never even arrives over the target."

"So let me get this straight. The planes we see in the sky are spraying chemicals into the atmosphere which are zapped by installations like HAARP to produce a layer of gunk which will neutralize the controls of any missile launched at the United States."

"That's it exactly and it works! This system was most likely what brought the cold war to an end and may have even led to the collapse of the Soviet Union in 1991."

"Here's what I don't understand. If this program is so wonderful, why all the hush-hush? I would think the politicians would be scrambling to take credit for the very thing that ended the nuclear threat."

He sighed. "That would be true except everything comes with a price. Like the ads for medications on TV, sometimes the side effects of something are far worse than the benefits and I'm afraid that's the case here."

"Are you talking about the screwed up weather patterns?"

"Among other things. Once this technology became known, the U.S. didn't have an exclusive on it. Today, not only the United States but also Russia, Canada and many European countries have installations similar to HAARP. With every major superpower bombarding and super heating the ionosphere to protect themselves from nuclear attack, there is no question it is altering the earth's weather patterns.

"Then there's the fallout. Whatever is sprayed up there, if it's heavier than air, will eventually fall to earth. That's another whole field of study.

"Unfortunately, that's not the end of it. Once directed spray into the atmosphere became an accepted practice, there have been a multitude of experiments, including the deployment of aerial vaccines."

"Holy crap! No wonder the government wants to keep this under wraps."

"Just curious," Katz said. "Why are you so interested in all this?"

I figured, *why not*, and told him what had transpired up to that moment. When I mentioned the photos, his eyes lit up.

"Really! May I see them?"

I pulled out my cell phone and flipped to the photos I had taken of the planes and the storage containers inside.

He clapped his hands like a little kid. "These are perfect! This is the final piece of the puzzle!"

"What puzzle?"

His eyes got a far-off look. "I've been collecting data on the chemtrail conspiracy for years. My intention was to publish a paper bringing the whole sordid affair out into the open, but there was always something missing, and now, here it is. Would you be willing to email those to me?"

"Of course!" He gave me his email address and it took just a few seconds to send them his way.

"Thank you so much! I'm eighty-five years old and I know my time on this old earth is limited, but I think I've got enough gas left in the old tank to put this paper together. This will be my parting shot --- my legacy!"

He glanced at his watch. "My goodness! I'm late for class. I must run. Thanks again!"

He gathered a stack of books and was out the door.

I was about to leave when a man I had seen at another table across the room approached.

He stuck out his hand. "I'm Dr. Evan Daniels, a professor here, and I don't mean to intrude but I couldn't help overhearing bits and pieces of your conversation. I hope you don't put too much stock in what my elderly colleague was telling you."

"Excuse me!"

"Dr. Katz. He's known around campus as Konspiracy Katz. He's been trying for years to get someone to listen to his wild theories about a covert government conspiracy which is filling our skies with poison."

I was immediately defensive. "Seems to me he had some pretty convincing evidence."

"What evidence? The thin, wispy clouds left behind by high-flying aircraft are known as contrails, short for condensation trails. These clouds are left behind as a result of the warm, moist exhaust of the plane's engines meeting the extremely cold temperatures of the upper atmosphere. It's a similar principle behind why you can see your breath on cold mornings. Contrails appear and disappear based on the moisture content of the air through which the plane is passing. If the upper atmospheric air is moist, the plane will leave a contrail which could last hours and spread out into a deck of cirrus. If the air is extremely dry, it might not leave a contrail at all.

"The year 1958 was a watershed year in commercial aviation. Boeing introduced the 707 and Douglas the DC-8, while a year later Convair debuted the 880. The turbojet engines on these airliners thrived in the cold thin air found above 30,000 feet and they were routinely operated in these flight levels. In the 1960's, contrails became commonplace across the United States, especially along designated jet airways between ground based navigation aids. When the temperature is low enough and the humidity high enough, the 1,500 gallons of water produced every hour by these jetliners was transformed into four cirrus clouds. When the humidity is very high, the contrails will remain for hours. In moderate humidity the contrails may last only a few seconds as the ice is absorbed into the atmosphere in a process known as sublimation. If the humidity is very low, the water vapor will immediately be absorbed into the atmosphere leaving the sky clear of contrails. Although the engines are producing numerous chemical compounds from the combustion of jet fuel, the only one which can be seen at altitude is H_2O in a frozen state. It's all really quite simple."

"Really! What about these?" I asked, showing him the photos on my phone.

"Ahhh, yes! The infamous storage containers for the deadly chemicals. Those pictures are of ballast tanks used in flight testing of new airliner designs. The tubes simply allow water to be pumped from tank to tank, simulating passenger motion in the cabin for the aircraft test."

He seemed to have an answer for everything.

"Before you go spreading Katz's daydreams, consider this. Both the Air Force and the Environmental Protection Agency have stated unequivocally there are no chemical or biological agents being deliberately released into our atmosphere."

"Well, if a government agency says so, it must be true," I replied with a hint of sarcasm. "Thanks for the tip."

As I walked back to my car, I was more confused than ever.

Everything Jack Carson, the Professor and Frank Katz had told me, while wildly speculative, had the ring of truth, but so did Evan Daniels' rebuttal.

Was I really dealing with a government conspiracy or was the whole thing just a paranoid delusion?

I knew I had to learn more before I could let it go.

CHAPTER 6

I hadn't heard from Jack Carson for a few days, so I figured I should give him a call and tell him what I'd learned at UMKC, from both Frank Katz and Evan Daniels. He deserved to hear both sides of the story.

I tried his office at the *Star* first and was told he was not available. Next, I tried his cell phone.

"This is Jack Carson. Who is this?"

The reception was poor and I could hear traffic in the background. "Walt Williams. Where in the world are you, Jack?"

"Highway 54, heading back to Kansas City. I've been to the Pinal Air Park in Marana, Arizona, the place where Falcon took the photos which were in his drawer. You wouldn't believe what I found."

"Try me."

"Before I left, I dug up as much as I could about the base. Turns out, it was owned and operated by the CIA during the Cold War and Vietnam, and served as a base of operations for many of their covert missions. Then it was sold to the Evergreen Company. The cover story was the airbase was to be kind of a graveyard for jets which were to be scrapped and it's true, there are hundreds of them waiting to be dismantled for parts. Evergreen also has a few tankers which the Forest Service uses to fight fires."

"Sounds pretty benign to me."

"That's what I thought until I got into the place. I was free to roam around and look at the derelicts, but then I spotted a gravel road which led to another more remote part of the facility. I finally came to a guard hut out in the middle of nowhere. The road was blocked by a barrier. A guard appeared out of the hut. I figured I must have stumbled onto some military installation, but the guard wasn't wearing a regular uniform. He was dressed in all-black para-military garb and carried an M4/M, M16 rifle. He told me in no uncertain terms this was a secured area, that I should turn around and never come back."

"I assume you did just that."

"You bet I did, but before I left, I saw the array of planes Falcon photographed in the distance."

"So did you get more photos?"

"Not then. The guard made me vamoose, so I got out of there and found a private aviation company and rented a helicopter for a couple of hours. The pilot didn't want to fly over the airbase, but finally relented when I opened my wallet. It cost me a bundle, but it was worth it."

"What did you see?"

"When we got over the part of the base which was restricted, I spotted a building that was built into the ground. The flat roof was camouflaged to look exactly like the surrounding desert, so it was very difficult to spot. I had just snapped a couple of photos when a black helicopter which looked exactly like the photos of the ones operated by the

CIA was on our tail. The moment the pilot spotted it, he turned and high-tailed it out of there. The black chopper followed us until we were far away from the base."

"I'll bet that was pretty intense."

"No kidding! Anyway, after we landed, I decided to ----. Hey! What the hell! Oh shit!"

Then the line went dead.

I tried to call him back but the call went straight to voice mail.

I sat for several minutes trying to decide what to do. Since I really had no idea where he was, I had just decided there wasn't much I could do when the phone rang.

"Walt, it's Jack again."

"Are you all right?"

"I guess so. Just shaken up. I'm out here in the middle of nowhere and some asshole runs me off the road. I was pretty lucky I guess. There was a real steep drop-off which went down to a dry creek bed. I was able to get stopped before I went over, otherwise, it would have been a long, bumpy ride to the bottom."

"I don't suppose the offending vehicle was a black SUV?"

"How did you ---? Oh, crap! Surely you're not thinking someone from the Air Base was trying to take me out."

"Think about it. You confronted an armed guard, then flew over restricted air space, and after that I'm guessing you stopped and tried to talk to people who lived near the base. Am I right?"

"Sure did, but nobody was talking. As soon as I mentioned the Air Base, people started slamming doors. Wow! I don't know why I'm surprised. Look what they did to Falcon."

"Allegedly did to Falcon."

"Yeah, right! Anything happening on your end?"

Carson got back on the road and while he was making his way back to Kansas City, I filled him in on my conversations with the Professor and Frank Katz as well as the rebuttal from Evan Daniels.

Carson was as excited as a kid on Christmas morning. "With everything we've got, how can anyone honestly deny the existence and purpose of the chemtrails?"

"What we have are a lot of opinions and no empirical evidence to back them up. I'm betting at this point anything you bring up can be explained away by someone like Evan Daniels. Without proof, your conspiracy theory is no more believable than sightings of Bigfoot or the Loch Ness Monster."

"Maybe so," he replied, "but I think I'm on to something big and I'm going to keep digging."

"Dig away, but just in case you're right, watch your back."

After hanging up from Carson, I was torn.

I knew I definitely wanted to know more about the wispy trails in the sky, but I also remembered the promise I'd made to Maggie. It wasn't a stretch to believe that if Carson was right, the SUV running him off the road probably wasn't an accident. The last thing in the world I wanted was to be the target of some black ops assassin.

I was pondering how I could get more information without drawing attention or ruffling feathers when it hit me --- Arnold Goldblume and Nicholas Thatcher.

I had met them several years earlier when I had been part of a Homeland Security team investigating people with terrorist ties in Kansas City.

Goldblume and Thatcher were part of a group known as the 'Watchers.' Their stated purpose was to be a watch dog organization keeping an eye on government shenanigans. They got Homeland Security's attention by sending emails which said things like, "I dropped my bomb pop and got it dirty." Since the emails contained the words 'bomb' and 'dirty', a covert program run by the government called Echelon, picked them up as terrorist threats for the deployment of a 'dirty bomb.'

Of course they weren't terrorists and Homeland Security agents had egg on their collective faces once it was discovered they were monitoring private citizen's emails.

The two met when they were part of a class action suit against the pharmaceutical company which made the drug Vioxx which had claimed the lives of both of their fathers.

The loss of their loved ones from a drug approved by the FDA fueled a suspicion of pretty much everything the government was up to, and the huge settlement they received funded their ongoing surveillance operations.

I figured if anyone had the inside skinny on the chemtrails, it would be them, and I could quiz them without worrying about reprisals from government assassins.

By the time our investigation was over, I had become friends with Arnie and Nick and an unofficial member of the Watchers, so when I called they were more than happy to have me drop by their office on Warwick Boulevard, a stone's throw away from the J.C. Nichols fountain where Arnie often held rallies to inform the public of the government's covert operations.

"Walt! So good to see you again," Arnie said as I walked in the door. "Nick, get your ass in here. We've got company."

When Nick joined his partner, I couldn't help wondering again at the remarkable resemblance they had to Simon and Garfunkle. Arnie was small and balding while Nick was gawky and gangly with a shock of unruly blonde hair.

They both gave me a hug and motioned me to a chair.

"So, to what do we owe the pleasure of your company?" Arnie asked.

"How much time to you have?" I replied.

"As much as you need, old friend. What's on your mind?"

I took a deep breath and told them everything. "So what's your take on all that?" I asked wrapping up my story. "Is there any truth to it or is this just another Elvis sighting?"

Nick and Arnie exchanged glances. "We've been preaching this for years, but nobody seems to give a damn. The trails in the sky have been there for so many years they're just a normal part of what most everyone has seen for their entire lives. They're so white and soft and fluffy. How could they possibly be dangerous? But make no mistake, those planes have been spewing poison into our atmosphere for years and now we're paying the price."

"Are you talking about the change in the weather patterns?"

"Absolutely! The droughts, the floods, the variations in the path of the jet stream --- they're all directly related to Project Cloverleaf and the bombardment of the ionosphere by HAARP, but that's just the tip of the iceberg. We're just now starting to feel the cumulative effects of the chemicals they've been spraying for years."

"What effects, exactly?"

Nick pulled a thick file folder from a cabinet. "It all started with the threat of global warming. The idea was to spray aluminum oxide into the atmosphere to reflect the sun's rays and reduce the steady rise in the earth's temperature.

"Once the technology for spraying the chemicals was perfected, the government think tank came up with the program we know as Operation Cloverleaf where ethylene dibromide, EDB, and barium are dispersed and then zapped by HAARP to make a defensive barrier to combat the threat of ICBM missiles."

Nick thumbed through some papers in the folder. "According to the Environmental Protection Agency, and I quote, 'Ethylene dibromide is a carcinogen and must be handled with extreme caution. A seven-page summary of this pesticide's extreme toxicity notes EDB may also damage the reproductive system. Exposure can irritate the lungs and repeated exposure may cause bronchitis, development of cough, and shortness of breath.'"

"But Evan Daniels said the EPA categorically denied chemicals are being sprayed into the atmosphere," I protested. "Surely the government wouldn't tell a bold-faced lie."

Arnie smiled ruefully. "You mean the same government that told us Agent Orange could defoliate a tropical jungle overnight but was harmless to humans? Just ask any Vietnam War vet how that turned out. The same government that told us nuclear power plants posed no danger? Ask anyone that lived within fifty miles of Chernobyl."

He wiped a tear from his eye. "The same government that told my father Vioxx was safe? Well, that was a lie, too, and now he's gone."

Nick quickly changed the subject. "Over the past decade, independent testing of the chemical fallout of atmospheric spraying around the country has shown a dangerous and extremely poisonous brew which includes nano sized aluminum particles, mercury, radioactive thorium, cadmium, chromium, nickel, desiccated blood, which may or may not contain a myriad of specific viruses, barium, mold spores, yellow fungal mycotoxins, ethylene dibromide, and other unidentified organic materials."

"Holy crap!"

"No kidding, and now all the stuff which has been sprayed over the years has accumulated on the ground, in the plants we eat and in all living organisms, and it's taking its toll."

"Have you heard about the disappearance of the bees?" Arnie asked, regaining his composure.

I nodded. I had read something about it in the Kansas City Star.

"It is estimated that one third of everything we eat was pollinated by bees, and now we discover the number of the little critters is declining by thirty percent in some areas and as much as eighty percent in other areas. Can you imagine the devastating effect this will have on our food supply in the future?

"Then there's the bats. In the past four years more than a million bats have died from a disease called white-nose syndrome.

"Ever heard of chronic wasting disease? It's a disease of the nervous system in deer and elk which results in distinctive brain lesions and death. It's estimated that already 25% of the herds are affected.

"There are massive fish kills all over the world and whales and dolphins are washing up on our shores in increasing numbers.

"Why, all of a sudden are these things happening? It's the cumulative effect of years of spraying poison in our skies that's finally taking its toll."

"Why in the world isn't something being done about this?" I asked in disbelief.

"Oh, someone is," Arnie replied. "Monsanto! They have applied for and been granted a patent to produce aluminum resistant seeds. At some point in time, the earth will simply be too toxic for natural plants to grow, so where will we turn? To Monsanto, of course, to save the day and provide seeds which will grow in toxic soil. Can anyone smell profit here?"

"Monsanto isn't the only company getting their foot in the door with the chemtrails," Nick added. "The huge pharmaceutical companies are lobbying for aerial disbursement of vaccines. The day may come when you'll be medicated whether you like it or not."

"So what's the answer to all this?" I asked, bewildered. "Why aren't the American people up in arms?"

The answer Arnie gave me was the same as the one given by the Professor --- apathy, frustration and complacency.

"If you gave this information to the average guy on the street, his response would probably be, 'Maybe it's true, maybe it isn't, but even if it is true, what could I do about it?' We've all been conditioned to believe government is just too big to fight."

"You still haven't given me an answer," I replied.

"Maybe what we need is another Edward Snowden," Nick said. "Some call him a traitor, some call him a hero and a patriot, but however you feel about him, we really didn't know how far the NSA was reaching into our private lives until he blew the whistle."

"Yeah, and look how that turned out for him."

"Yes, there is that, but nothing's going to happen with these chemtrails until someone with first-hand knowledge comes forward to expose what's going on."

I silently wondered if Jack Carson would be that person.

CHAPTER 7

After my meeting with Arnie and Nick, I was totally confused.

What they had to say, added to what I had learned from the Professor, Frank Katz and Jack Carson, pointed to a covert government operation which affected every American.

I went to the Internet to get more information on the subject and discovered there were HUNDREDS of sites supporting the notion that the chemtrails were part of an ongoing government program.

What I also found were almost as many sites debunking the conspiracy theory and offering alternative theories to that hypothesis.

One site would say the streaks in the sky are chemicals being spewed into the atmosphere for clandestine purposes. Then another site would explain why they are nothing more than water condensation produced by the big jets which has turned to ice crystals in the frigid upper atmosphere.

One site would show photos like the one I found in Falcon's apartment, claiming the big tanks in the belly of the aircraft contain the chemicals, while another site would say what we are seeing are ballast tanks used in flight testing of new airliner designs.

One site would show photos of massive fish kills, saying the thousands of dead fish are caused by the cumulative effect of the chemicals which have been sprayed and fallen to earth over the years, while another site would claim the kills are caused by El Nino and global warming.

Are the trails in the sky a conspiracy or just paranoid delusions?

There were convincing arguments on both sides. The answer depended on who you wanted to believe.

I let my mind wander for a moment and examined the possibility that the chemtrail theorists were correct.

Just a few short years ago, it was unthinkable to believe our government was listening to our phone conversations and reading our emails, but it proved to be true.

When the NSA was caught with their hands in the cookie jar, they justified their action by citing the hundreds of terrorist attacks that were thwarted, and the many thousands of lives which were saved as a result of their snooping. A typical case of the ends justifying the means.

I can only imagine the discussion that might have taken place in some secluded room years ago.

"Shall we ask the people of our country for permission to invade their privacy or just go ahead and do it? After all it's for their own good."

We know what was ultimately decided and why. The chances were slim and none the average

American wanted Big Brother snooping in their lives.

I could see a similar scenario with the chemtrails.

Years ago, our government was faced with two huge problems, global warming and the Russian ICBM's pointed at the U.S. If they believed spraying chemicals into the atmosphere was the answer to these threats, it was highly unlikely they would go to the American people and ask permission to spray poison into the air. The average guy on the street just wouldn't understand. Sure, there would be consequences, but certainly nothing as devastating as a nuclear bomb exploding in New York City or Los Angeles. The ends justified the means.

On a much more basic level, I could remember my parent's admonitions to not run with scissors, not stick beans up my nose or ride my bike with no hands, and I remember protesting, "WHY?"

The answer would always be, "Because I told you so! It's for your own good."

It's no secret those in positions of power often make authoritarian decisions because they believe it's for the greater good.

Or, on the other hand, maybe the fluffy trails in the sky are just ice crystals.

These were the thoughts running through my mind when I met my dad and Bernice, his significant other, returning to their respective apartments on the second floor of my building.

They didn't seem to be their chipper selves. "Why so glum?" I asked.

Dad just shrugged. "We went to see Doc Johnson. We've both been a bit under the weather. Stuffy noses, aches and pains, not much energy."

"So what did he say?"

"Not much. He said it wasn't the flu. He wondered if we had been around other people our age. I told him we go to the tea dance at the Senior Center every week. He said we might have caught something there. He'd been seeing a lot of seniors lately with the same symptoms. Hell, maybe it's just old age. We're both ninety."

"So what did he tell you to do?"

"Go home, drink lots of fluids and get some rest, so that's what we're going to do."

Then I saw a twinkle in his eye. "I'm going to whip up a pitcher of margaritas, then Bernice and I are going to hop into bed."

"I'm not sure that's what Doc Johnson had in mind. What about rest?"

"We'll rest afterward," he replied, patting Bernice on the rear end.

As they headed off, I was reminded of my visit with Arnie and Nick. They had shown me an article by a Doctor Len Horowitz. The article stated exposure to ethylene dibromide, the stuff that was supposed to be a major component in the chemtrails, could result in general weakness, vomiting, diarrhea, chest pains, coughing, shortness of breath, upper respiratory tract

68

irritation and respiratory failure caused by swelling of the lymph glands in the lungs. The article stated that the elderly and people with compromised immune systems were particularly vulnerable.

It was certainly something to consider, or maybe, it was just old age.

I had just settled into my recliner when the phone rang.

"Walt, it's Jack. I'm back in town and we need to talk. Can you meet me at Mel's Diner in a half hour?"

"Are you buying?"

A big sigh. "Yes, yes, I'll buy."

"See you there."

When I arrived, there were already two huge pieces of pie and two steaming cups of coffee on the table.

"A man of your word," I said, approvingly. Then I noticed a red knot on the side of his head. "What happened to you?"

"Bumped my head when that jackass ran me off the road. It could have been a lot worse."

"So no other incidents on your way home?"

"Nope. I'm hoping it was just some drunk or maybe someone texting while driving. It's just scary as hell thinking I might be the target of a government assassin."

"Yeah, I get that. Let me tell you about a meeting I had with a couple of friends."

I proceeded to tell him about the Watchers and my visit with Arnie and Nick.

Needless to say, he was enthusiastic. "Just another nail in their coffin. The more I hear, the more I smell Pulitzer Prize in this story."

If you live to write it, I thought. "So what's next?"

"Ever hear of Kristen Meghan?"

I shook my head. "Can't say I have."

"She worked for the Federal Government for twelve years, nine of which was with the Air Force as a bio-environmental engineer. Auditing chemicals used by the military was part of her responsibility. She found a hanger full of drums filled with the stuff we've been talking about, ethylene dibromide, and so on. The chemicals weren't tied to any known operation, so she started investigating.

"She had heard of the chemtrail conspiracy and started out with the goal of proving the chemicals weren't tied to any kind of covert operation, but instead, she discovered just the opposite. Soil testing in various locations were found to have significantly higher amounts of the chemicals which were in the drums. The only way they could have been dispersed that broadly was through the air.

"In 2012, she went public with what she knew According to her, the military threatened to lock her up and take away her daughter if she didn't stop asking questions."

"Let me guess," I said. "You're going to pay her a visit."

"I am. I'm hoping she'll be willing to talk to me and maybe even share some of the test results from her studies. It would be one more bit of evidence to add to everything I've found so far."

"Well, good luck with that, and just in case you were wrong about the drunk driver, watch your back."

"Will do," he said, and was out the door.

When I first arrived at the diner, I spotted a man in another booth with a lap top computer. I didn't pay much attention to him at first, but after Jack and I had talked for over an hour, the guy was still sitting there.

When I got up to leave, he hadn't moved.

I got in my car and was halfway home when it struck me. I made a u-turn and headed back to the diner.

The guy with the computer was gone.

I went inside and flagged Mel who was busy scraping his huge flat, cast iron grill. I had been a regular customer for years and considered Mel a good friend.

"More pie?" he asked.

"No. That guy, the one sitting in that booth with the lap top. Was he one of your regular customers?"

"Nope, never seen him before."

"He was certainly here a long time."

"He sure as hell was, and the piker didn't even leave a tip."

Could have been anybody, I thought, *Maybe he was a student from the university.*

Then again, maybe not.

CHAPTER 8

The next morning, I had a welcome respite from my stewing over the chemtrail dilemma --- my wife needed me.

Now that I'm seventy-two it's not often a woman, especially one as fetching as my wife, says she has need of my services, so I make it a point to be available.

For twenty-five years, I was a real estate agent. At age sixty-five, I traded my briefcase for a badge. Maggie and I both worked at City Wide Realty. In fact, that's where we met. Maggie's still an agent and a very good one. Because of her experience and her sterling work ethic, the broker, Dave Richards, often gives Maggie some of the trickier listings.

It was exactly that scenario that prompted her to ask if I had plans for the morning. Luckily, I did not.

The listing Dave had given her was a large estate on Sunset Drive just south of the Country Club Plaza. Hector Ramirez who was the Kansas City contact for a Columbian Drug cartel had owned it until the Drug Task Force shut down his operation.

As is often the case, the government confiscates property seized under these circumstances. Ramirez' trial had taken the better part of a year and the house had sat vacant until the guilty verdict was rendered.

One reason Dave gives these gems to Maggie is she has a team of workers ready to turn the neglected estate into a showplace. Consuela and her two daughters clean the place from top to bottom, Larry the Landscaper trims the shrubs and mows the lawn, and Jeff the Bugman exterminates the creepy crawlers lurking in the cracks and crevices. John, the licensed home inspector, goes through the entire home and gives Maggie a list of everything which needs repaired. The list is then given to Freddie the Fix-it guy, and before you know it, the place is ready for the cover of *Better Homes and Gardens*.

This morning was to be Maggie's first visit to the vacant house to take measurements and to make notes to give to her crew.

Maggie and I have a rule that says she never EVER goes to a vacant house alone. Six years ago, she was abducted and barely escaped with her life. We never want that to happen again.

When we pulled up in front of the house, there was no doubt her crew would have their hands full.

The grass, having not been mowed for a year, was as high as an elephant's eye as Gordon MacRae used to sing in one my favorite musicals, *Oklahoma*.

As Maggie slipped the key into the door lock, I noticed a furry creature scramble for cover under the porch.

The stench which slapped us in the face when we stepped inside brought tears to our eyes. The dead rat at the foot of the second floor staircase probably didn't help. Jeff the Bugman, when stepping into such an odoriferous dwelling, often remarks that the place smells like ass-crack. I had never argued the point.

"Holy crap, Maggie. Can your crew really turn this into a saleable listing?"

She gave an involuntary shudder. "If anyone can, it's them. Well, we might as well get started. This place isn't going to measure itself."

I switched on my flashlight. All the utilities had been turned off and that was another reason we had to hang around the stinky place for a couple of hours. The utility companies were all scheduled to arrive at some point to turn things on.

Maggie had one of those electronic gizmos which she holds up to the wall and when a button is pushed, the distance to the other wall is displayed. Just another example of the technological advances since I started measuring houses years ago with a retractable tape.

My job was to hold the flashlight and then record the room's measurements as Maggie read the meter. We were making good time since the rooms were virtually empty, the Drug Task Force having removed and sold anything of value.

Things were proceeding nicely until we reached the kitchen. While I was waiting for Maggie to take the first reading, I made the huge mistake of opening the refrigerator door.

Whoever had cleaned out the place had neglected to remove the food items from the fridge and they had an entire year, sealed up in the hot interior, to morph into God only knew what. The fridge's innards were a veritable petri dish of fungus and black mold.

Trying to stifle my gag reflex, I slammed the door shut, but it was too late, the room filled with the fumes of rotting decay.

It was at that moment, the guy from Kansas City Power and Light made his appearance. He stepped into the room and coughed. "Crimeny! It smells like ass-crack in here!"

If two guys say it, it must be true.

He turned the power on, but of course after a year, the a/c didn't work, so we spent the next four hours sweating like pigs. At last, all the rooms had been measured and all the utilities had been turned on. Maggie hung a lock box on the door and we headed for home.

Once inside, I said jokingly, "I'll flip you to see who gets the shower first."

She thought for a moment, then said, "Tell you what. You went way beyond the call of duty today and I owe you. How about we take that shower together?"

"I don't know," I replied teasingly. "Will you wash my back?"

"I'll wash anything you want," she said demurely.

"You'll even wash my ---?"

"Oh, shut up and get in here," she said taking my hand.

On the way to the bathroom, I noticed the message light on the phone was blinking.

It'll wait, I thought, thinking of my sudsy reward for a job well done.

Forty-five minutes later, after the water had run cold, I was toweling dry, when I remembered the phone message.

I hit the 'play' button and an obviously excited voice came on the line.

"Walt, this is Frank Katz. I just wanted you to know I finished my thesis on the chemtrails and I'm not too modest to say it's brilliant. As soon as I add a few finishing touches, I'll be submitting it to several publications. I'm convinced that once this information is in print, the public will simply not be able to ignore the trails crisscrossing our sky. They're going to demand answers from our government. Soon, just like the snooping of the NSA, their dirty little secrets will be revealed for all to see. As soon as it's in print, I'll send you a copy. Thanks again for your input."

Frank Katz was about to hurl a stone at a hornet's nest. It would be interesting to see who got stung.

CHAPTER 9

At seven the next morning, I struggled out of bed and headed to the kitchen for my coffee and bowl of Wheaties, the breakfast of champions. After our exhausting day at Maggie's new listing, I had planned to just take it easy, stay at home and catch up on some paperwork. I was, after all, supposed to be retired.

But it wasn't to be.

I had just opened the morning paper when the phone rang. It was Mary, the housemother at my Three Trails Hotel.

"Mr. Walt, if you ain't busy I wonder if you could come over?"

"Problems?"

"Not exactly. I got a kid wanting to rent a room and, well, he's not like all the others."

"How so?"

"He seems like a sharp kid and it don't make no sense, him wanting to live in this dump."

A lot of folks would take offense at someone calling their property a dump, but not me. I had accepted that description years ago.

A charitable description of the Three Trails would be 'flop house.' There are twenty sleeping rooms which share four hall baths, not a good ratio if several of the tenants get the squirts at the same time.

I understood what Mary was saying. Most of the residents were old dudes on Social Security or high school dropouts working out of the day labor pool.

The last tenant who didn't fit the usual description was Lawrence Wingate. The poor fellow had gone into the hospital for a life threatening operation. Before doing so, he gave his wife full power of attorney in case he didn't make it off the table. By the time he woke up from the anesthesia, his wife had sold their home, cleaned out their bank accounts and run off to Hawaii with her secret lover. When the poor guy got out of the hospital, the Three Trails was all he could afford.

"Sure, I can come over," I said, folding up my paper. Best laid plans and all that.

"Bring Willie, too," she added. "I need some bulbs replaced and my old bones just don't feel like climbing a ladder today."

Mary was tough as nails. She had to be to keep the guys at the hotel in line, but she was seventy-something and old age was beginning to creep up on her.

"Will do. See you in twenty minutes."

I gave Willie a call and asked him to meet me on the front porch.

Before I retired from real estate, I owned over two hundred apartment units and Willie was in charge of maintenance. Over the years, we became fast friends and when I sold the buildings and got out of the rental business, Willie kind of retired with me. I give him a studio apartment in the basement of my building rent free for taking care of the odd jobs around our building and the hotel.

Willie beat me to the porch. "Trouble at de hotel?" he asked, getting slowly to his feet. Willie, like me, was seventy-two, and wasn't as spry as he used to be.

"No trouble. Mary just wants some light bulbs changed and wants me to meet a new tenant. It shouldn't take long."

"Dat's good, cause I'd planned to spend some time wif Emma today."

Although his body was feeling the effects of Father Time, apparently his libido was not.

When we arrived at the hotel, Mary and the young man she'd called about were sitting on the porch swing chatting.

"Walt, this is Billy Campbell. He wants to rent a room. I thought you'd like to meet him. Billy, this is Mr. Walt. He owns the place."

Campbell jumped to his feet and extended his hand. "Pleased to meet you, Sir."

I saw right away what Mary was talking about. The guy was clean shaven, his hair was trimmed and his clothes were spotless. As far as I could recall, he was the first prospective tenant to ever call me Sir.

"Nice to meet you too. If you don't mind me asking, this place isn't exactly the Ritz. You look like you could afford better."

"Oh, I could, but most places want me to sign a lease, and to be honest, I'm not sure how long I'll be in town. Mary said you rent by the week and that's perfect for me. I might be here one week, maybe two. It depends on how things work out."

"Looking for work?"

He hesitated. "Uhhh, yes, work. If I find a job, I might stay longer."

I turned to Mary. "I don't see a problem. Why don't you get one of our applications and we'll get Mr. Campbell settled in."

I saw the confused look on her face. We actually did have an application form, but had quit using it years ago. Basically, if a guy was breathing and had the forty bucks for the first week, he was in.

"Just get the form, Mary. I have a pen."

Billy Campbell filled out the form and Mary gave him his key. "Number 6. Top of the stairs, third door on the right."

Billy took the key, picked up his duffel and headed up to his room.

Mary was about to ask me why I wanted the application, when the front door burst open and Oscar Biddle from #18 came stomping out.

"You've got to do something about him!" he bellowed.

"Who?"

"Old man Feeney. He stopped up the #3 crapper again. Smells like ass-crack in there."

I had been hearing that a lot lately, but this actually made sense.

I saw Willie roll his eyes. "I'll take care of it, but if I was actually gettin' paid for dis job, I'd be wantin' me some hazardous duty pay."

I tucked the application and the pen in my pocket and waited for Willie on the porch swing.

I tried to time my arrival at the crime lab between shifts. I was going to ask for a favor and the fewer people who knew, the better.

Bernie Morton was hunched over a microscope, feverishly making notes. He looked up when he heard me at the door.

"Well, well, it's the aged half of the dynamic duo," he said, referring to the moniker the squad had bestowed on Ox and me. "How's retirement?"

"I wouldn't know. I can't quite get a handle on sitting around doing nothing."

"So I've heard. Got your own P.I. business. What brings you by?"

"I need a favor."

I saw him roll his eyes. "Walt, as much as I like you, you know I can't ---."

"Not even for a date with a special young lady?"

He looked at me skeptically. "Who, exactly?"

"Little Debbie," I replied, pulling a box of the snack cakes out of a grocery bag. It was common knowledge around the precinct that he was a sucker for the tasty treats.

"What would I have to do?"

"Nothing earth shattering. I've got a fingerprint I'd like you to run." I said, pulling the pen I'd wrapped in a sandwich bag out of my pocket.

"That's all?" he asked, glancing around to see if anyone was looking.

"That's it," I replied.

He grabbed Little Debbie out of my hand. "Give me the pen."

A few moments later, he had a clean print. "This could take a while," he said.

"Then let me save us both some time," I replied. "Start with the military database."

The 'Sir' and the military buzz cut made it a good bet my new tenant had been in one of the branches of the armed services.

He punched some keys and five minutes later, he pumped his fist. "Bingo! We've got a match."

I looked at the screen, and sure enough, there was my new tenant.

"The name's Charles Harris," he said, scrolling down the screen, "And guess what!"

"What?"

"The guy's AWOL."

"What branch of the service?"

"Air Force."

"Does it say where he's stationed?"

He scrolled some more. "Yep, Pinal Air Base in Marana, Arizona."

Suddenly, everything made sense,

"Thanks, Bernie," I said, hustling out the door. "Don't be too hard on Little Debbie."

I didn't understand his reply. His mouth was already full.

When I pulled up in front of the hotel, I wasn't exactly sure what I was going to do. I was about to confront a member of the armed services who was a hell of a lot younger and stronger than me.

I knew the prudent thing would be to call the local Air Force office and tell them what I knew, but something held me back. I had an idea, and if I was right, calling his superiors was the worst thing I could do. If I was wrong, I was probably in for the ass-whipping of my life.

I took a deep breath and headed up the stairs.

I knocked.

"Who's there?"

"Walt Williams, the landlord. We met earlier."

"Sure," he said, opening the door. What can I do for you, Sir?"

"We need to talk, Charles."

The moment of truth had arrived.

I half expected a fist in the face, but instead, he stepped aside. "How did you know?"

"I used to be a cop," I replied. "Your cover story was good, but your 'Sir' and your buzz cut gave you away. It's not easy shedding years of military training. If my information is correct, you're AWOL and people are looking for you."

"Are you going to turn me in?"

"That depends on what you tell me in the next five minutes. You were stationed at Pinal Air Base in Arizona?"

He nodded.

"I don't suppose you knew a pilot named Dale Fox?"

I saw the look of astonishment register on his face. "How --- how did you know that?"

"Well, did you?"

"Hell yes I knew him. I was a member of his flight crew. If you knew Dale, then you know he's dead."

"Is that why you ran?"

He sighed and nodded. "We were doing some pretty weird stuff out there. We were told our missions were classified and we were not to talk about them to anyone. They said it was a matter of national security. Dale knew a lot more about the missions than I did.

"He told me one day he was going to talk to a reporter. I tried to talk him out of it. Our commanding officer had made it clear that doing something like that would have dire consequences."

"So why are you running? You didn't spill the beans."

"Because I knew he was going to do it and I didn't report it to my commanding officer. As far as they're concerned, I'm just as guilty. When I heard Dale was dead, I figured I was next."

"So what's your plan? I'm sure you know if they catch you, you'll be spending a lot of years in Leavenworth."

"I figure three things could happen. I could disappear and they never would find me, or they could catch me and I'd go to prison. Either of those two things would be better than the third alternative."

"What's that?"

"What they did to Dale."

He looked me in the eye. "So, are you going to turn me in?"

"I probably should, but I won't. Will you promise me one thing?"

"Anything."

"Wherever you wind up, if you see national headlines exposing the missions at Pinal Air Base, you'll call me so we can talk."

"I promise."

"Good luck and God speed," I said, leaving the distraught young airman sitting on a lumpy mattress in a fleabag hotel. I'm sure this wasn't the way he had pictured his military career ending.

The next morning, Mary called. "Mr. Walt, Billy Campbell, the young man you met yesterday, he moved out in the middle of the night. He paid for a full week and only stayed one night. He didn't even ask for a refund."

I probably wouldn't have either.

CHAPTER 10

A few days later, I was once again pouring over the *Kansas City Star* in between spoonsful of Wheaties and sips of coffee. I'm very set in my ways and once I find something that suits me, I stick with it.

Maggie says I'm stuck in a rut, but doing the same thing over and over saves a lot of decision making. Once in a while I'll fool her and whip up a batch of hotcakes.

For some reason, maybe because I'm seventy-two, I always glance through the obituaries. Once in a while I'll spot the name of an old classmate or someone I knew years earlier. My tenant Jerry says he reads the obits and if his name isn't there, it's going to be a good day.

I was going down the list when a name jumped out and smacked me in the face.

Frank Katz was dead.

The listing gave his age as eighty-two and talked about his lengthy tenure at the university. He was survived by one granddaughter, Samantha Stewart.

I folded the paper under my arm and headed down to the Professor's apartment. I figured since he hadn't called me, he probably hadn't heard about the demise of his old friend. I didn't want to break the news over the phone.

As I expected, he hadn't heard and the news came as quite a shock.

"So sad," he said. "I talked to Frank just last week. He was so excited about finishing his thesis."

"Yes, he called me, too. I'd like to know more about how he died. The paper says he had one granddaughter, Samantha. By any chance do your know her, maybe have her phone number?"

"Yes, I believe I do. When I was still teaching, Sam would pop into the teacher's lounge every now and then, and I saw her at school functions. Let me see if I can find her number."

After a few minutes, he returned and handed me a slip of paper. "When you talk to Sam, please give her my condolences. Her father was a great teacher and an even greater friend."

I hadn't mentioned it to the Professor, but I had the nagging feeling there was more to Frank Katz' death than was reported in the paper. Was it just a coincidence Dale Fox was about to give hard evidence of the chemtrail conspiracy to Jack Carson, but died in a car wreck before he could deliver the goods, and now Frank Katz is dead after completing a thesis which would expose the government's dirty little chemtrail secrets? I was willing to bet he passed away before he could submit his thesis for publication. Unlucky coincidence? I didn't think so.

I desperately wanted to talk to Samantha Stewart, but I had another call to make first.

"Ox, this is Walt. Are you still at the precinct?"

"Hi Partner. We were just leaving."

"Can you do me a favor before you go?"

"Sure, name it."

"Two days ago, a Frank Katz passed away. The paper didn't say where he died. Could you find the report from the attending officers?"

"I'll take a look and call you back."

Ten minutes later, the phone rang.

"Walt, I've got it. It says a student at the university stopped by Frank Katz' office early that day and found him sitting at his desk, stone cold dead. There was no sign of foul play and Katz' doctor said the old guy had a bum ticker, so it was ruled a natural death, probably a heart attack, and the body was released to the next of kin."

"Thanks, that's just what I needed."

"Why the interest?"

"It's a long story. Maybe you and Judy can come over this weekend and I'll fill you in."

"Sounds like a plan. I'll have Judy give Maggie a call."

Heart attack. Pretty convenient.

I had just finished a case where a sadistic s.o.b. was murdering patients in the cardiac wing of one of the city's large hospitals. He would sneak in after hours and inject potassium chloride into their I.V. line while they were sleeping. The drug stops the heart and mimics the symptoms of a heart attack. Since the patients were all there because of heart problems, it was assumed they died of natural causes.

I needed to get to Samantha Stewart and persuade her to have an autopsy done on her father's body to look for injection marks and the presence of potassium chloride in his system.

grand

After explaining I was a friend of the Professor, Samantha Stewart agreed to meet with me.

Her home on Brookside Boulevard was just a stone's throw from the university.

She greeted me warmly and invited me inside.

"So how do you know the Professor?"

"I'm a UMKC graduate and I took a number of his classes. He became somewhat of a mentor to me. When he retired, he rented an apartment in my building on Armour Boulevard. I live on the third floor, he lives on the first. He asked me to convey his condolences on the passing of your grandfather."

"Please give him my thanks. He and Granddad were such good friends."

"About your grandfather, I know he supposedly died of natural causes, but I just wonder if you considered asking for an autopsy."

I saw the confused look on her face. "Why in the world would I do that? Dr. Friedman said it was most likely a heart attack."

I didn't want to alarm her. "It probably was. By any chance did you know what your grandfather was working on?"

"Not for sure. I know he was really excited about some paper he had just finished. You know how people in academic circles are, the old 'publish or perish' rule. He was eighty-two. I don't know why he was so concerned about being published at his age."

"So he never told you what the paper was about?"

"Never, and even if he did, I probably wouldn't have understood a word of it."

"He actually called me a week or so ago. I had given him some information he used in his thesis and he was telling me he was getting ready to submit it for publication. It was really an important document. I don't suppose you'd know where it is?"

She thought for a moment. "It had to be either in his home office or his office at the university. Someone from the Arts and Sciences Department came by the day after his death and wanted to know if I would be willing to donate his paperwork and files to the university. They said something about cataloging them in the Linda Hall Library on the campus. Frankly, I was relieved. He had several file cabinets full of stuff and I had no idea what to do with all of it. So either way, the people at the university must have it."

"Back to the autopsy ---."

She held up her hand to stop me. "I still don't understand why you think an autopsy is necessary, but it's actually a moot point."

"Why is that?"

"Because Granddad was cremated. He wanted it that way."

My heart sunk. I would have bet anything an autopsy would have revealed potassium chloride in his system, but now we would never know.

I knew I wasn't going to get anything more from Samantha Stewart, so I thanked her for her time and left.

My next stop was at the Arts and Sciences building on the UMKC campus.

A secretary announced my presence to the head of the department, Arnold Gregory.

"I have a few moments before a staff meeting, Mr. Williams. How may I help you?"

"I have a few questions about Frank Katz."

"Ahh, yes. Poor Frank. Such a loss. He will be missed."

"I understand your department has collected his papers and files to be catalogued into the Linda Hall Library."

"Who told you that?"

"His granddaughter, Samantha Stewart."

"I can't imagine why she'd say such a thing. The only contact I've had with Mrs. Stewart was to offer our condolences."

I couldn't believe what I was hearing.

"How about his office here at the university?"

"There was not much there, not even a computer. He's done most of his work at his home office these past few years."

Another dead end.

Someone had contacted Samantha Stewart claiming to be from the university and cleaned out the old guy's office which undoubtedly held the damning manuscript.

It didn't take a rocket scientist to guess who had orchestrated the whole thing.

I was totally bummed.

Two men were gone, along with all the evidence they had collected to expose the government's poisoning of our skies.

It was becoming quite apparent the people behind these dastardly acts would stop at nothing to keep their program under wraps.

I had planned to go home, pour a glass of Arbor Mist and try to decide what I should do next.

I knew I had to contact Jack Carson and tell him of this latest development, but beyond that I should probably do nothing, because that's what I'd promised Maggie.

I stopped at the mailbox and found it stuffed full of bills. It was that time of the month. I had already decided my involvement in the chemtrail case should come to an end, so I resigned myself to an afternoon of bill paying.

Since retiring from real estate, I was rarely on the computer. Social media just wasn't my thing. I didn't have an account on Facebook, Twitter, or any of the other message sites. Every few days I would log on to check my email and I had learned to pay my bills online, saving me the agony of handwriting checks and paying for first class postage.

I fired up the old Toshiba and was about to log on to my bank account when the butler strolled across my screen and announced, "You have mail, Sir."

I figured I might as well look so he would go away.

There was the usual stuff, a message from a guy in Nigeria saying he needed to get twenty million dollars out of the country and he'd split it with me if I would just send him my bank account information. Then there was the ad for a product promising to add three inches to my penis. I thought about getting that and surprise Maggie, but decided against it. I'd have to buy bigger briefs and I don't like to shop.

The next email definitely caught my eye. It was from Frank Katz and it had a .pdf attachment.

The message read, "Walt, after our conversation the other day, I decided to send you a copy of my manuscript. Please take a look at it and if you have any suggestions, please let me know before I submit it for publication." The time stamp was the evening before he was found dead the next morning.

I opened the file and read the document. As promised, it was a scathing exposé of everything Katz had collected about the chemtrail conspiracy. While lacking in actual physical evidence, there was certainly enough circumstantial evidence to raise some eyebrows. Apparently enough evidence *hat* someone had taken extraordinary measures to see it never saw the light of day.

Then the reality hit me like a thunderbolt. The original manuscript was long gone and I most likely had the only other copy.

If my theory was correct, Frank Katz had died because of the very thing which was staring at me from my computer screen.

I had promised Maggie I would steer clear of this thing so as not to endanger ourselves, our family and our friends, but no matter how hard I tried to distance myself, I kept getting sucked back in.

What was I to do with it? There was no way in hell I was going to try to get it published myself and bring the wrath of some assassin to our door. I thought about giving it to Jack Carson. He was, after all, a journalist and had the perfect venue to share the information with the world. Then I remembered the incident with the SUV when he was returning from Arizona. Undoubtedly, Carson was already on these people's radar. Sending him the document might just sign his death warrant. I wanted no part of that.

What I needed was a way to get the information out to the public in a non-threatening way which wouldn't put the writer at risk.

Then it hit me. If the information in Katz' thesis was published as a work of fiction, it would be out there for the world to see and people would be made aware of the possibility of a government conspiracy and it just might open some eyes.

What I needed was a successful novelist and I knew just the right guy, Robert Thornhill.

I had met him a few months ago at a craft fair. We had received information that terrorists had planted explosives at the event that put the lives of nearly a thousand people in danger. Using drug dogs from the K-9 Corps, we found the bombs. We subdued one of the bad guys immediately, but the second one broke for the door. His escape route took him right past the table where Thornhill was displaying his books. With perfect timing, Thornhill flipped the table on its side spewing a hundred slick paperback books in the terrorist's path. The perp was down just long enough for the cops to pounce and put him in cuffs.

After the incident we talked. Thornhill had published twenty mystery novels, a few of them based on cases which Ox and I had been involved in. Evidently he had a large fan base as eight of his works had hit #1 on Amazon during the previous year.

We found another common bond. We had both experienced open heart surgery and were actually on the cardiac floor of St. Luke's Hospital at the same time.

He autographed several of his books for me. I offered to pay him, but he declined and said I could pay him by sharing more stories to fuel his imagination.

I figured this might be the perfect time to repay my debt.

We had exchanged contact information and I had his number in my phone.

He picked up on the second ring.

"Mr. Thornhill, this is Walt Williams. Would you have a few minutes to talk?"

"Walt! Good to hear from you. Of course I'd love to chat with you, but let's not be formal. Please call me Bob."

"Well, Bob, I just might have a story that would pique your interest."

"You have my attention. What have you got?"

"Not on the phone. Could we meet somewhere?"

"Sure, how about lunch at Mel's Diner, say eleven-thirty?"

I was pleasantly surprised by his choice of eating establishments. "Sounds good to me. I'll see you there."

Bob was right on time. We met in the parking lot and entered together. Mel glanced up from his grill when we entered.

"Hi Bob. Hi Walt."

I was surprised again. "You two know each other?"

"Of course," Mel replied. "Bob's a regular. Hamburger patty, grilled onions and fries, and I suppose you'll want the chicken fried steak?"

We both nodded. Mel was amazing.

"I've been coming here for years," I said. "It's a wonder we've never bumped into each other before."

"Well, we're here now, and I can't wait to hear what you have for me."

I started at the beginning and told Bob everything I knew about the conspiracy and had just finished when Mel brought huge pieces of his chocolate cream pie. Bob had listened intently and taken notes, only interrupting sporadically to ask for clarification on some point.

When I finished, Bob just shook his head. "Holy crap, Walt! This is one ugly can of worms you've opened. Why, exactly, are you telling me all of this?"

"I'm telling you because I want this to be the subject of your next novel."

"Really! You've just told me two men are dead trying to expose this conspiracy and now you're dumping it in my lap?"

"But this is different. You write fiction. I've read all kinds of books about corrupt politicians, government conspiracies and secret spy missions, and to my knowledge, none of the authors have been whacked yet."

"*Yet*, being the operative word here."

Bob thought for a moment. "So far, I've written about vigilantism, euthanasia, and the collusion between the FDA and the pharmaceutical giants without reprisal. Maybe I could get by with one

100

more. Although I often wonder if I'm on some CIA watch list. When I wrote about the Avenging Angels, I had to learn how to make a bomb just like the one Timothy McVeigh used to blow up the Federal Building in Oklahoma City. It's all right there on the Internet, every detail. I could only imagine some government program set up to monitor the computers of people looking up that stuff."

"So are you in?" I asked expectantly.

He smiled. "Sure, why not? I'm just a retired seventy-two year old guy who writes mystery novels for the fun of it. What could possibly be the danger in that?"

That's probably what Frank Katz believed too, I thought, but I didn't say it out loud.

I handed Bob the manuscript which I had downloaded on a thumb drive. "Here it is. Good luck. I'll be anxious to read the finished product."

I headed back home, determined to finish my bill paying which was interrupted by Frank Katz' email.

I booted up the computer, but instead of my usual screensaver, there was nothing but squiggly lines. I turned the thing off and restarted it. That often cured the anomalies which sometimes popped up, but this time, it didn't work. No matter what I tried, all I could get was the same squiggly lines.

I was totally frustrated and had slumped back in my chair trying to figure out what to do when I noticed something strange. The stack of bills I was going to tackle was not where I had left them. They weren't moved much, but just enough so it got my attention.

I picked up the phone and dialed Maggie.

"Hi, Sweetie."

"Maggie, by any chance did you come home for lunch?"

"No, Anita and I had a salad at the Panera Bread Company. I haven't been home since I left this morning. Why do you ask?"

I didn't want to alarm her. "No reason, really. I was out myself and just wondered if I'd missed you. See you later."

I hung up before she could quiz me further.

I headed out the door and met Dad in the hall.

"Dad, have you seen any strangers in the halls today?"

He thought for a moment. "Strangers? No, not really. Just the guy from the gas company. He said they were checking all the buildings on the block for leaks. I sent him down to Willie. That's the last I saw of him."

I thanked him and headed to the basement.

"Willie, did you talk to a gas man today?"

"Sho did. De man said he was lookin' for de gas line an' I showed him where it was. He had one of those sniffer things with him. He poked around for a few minutes, den said everything was fine an' left."

I headed back to my apartment.

Gas man, my ass!

I unplugged my computer and headed to Arnie and Nick's place on Warwick.

Nick was the computer nerd and I knew if anyone could fix it, it would be him.

I brought the two of them up to date and handed Nick my laptop.

He booted it up, punched some keys and frowned. "Sorry, Walt. Your hard drive is corrupted, totally fried, probably a virus of some kind."

"But how? I've got virus protection software installed."

"It doesn't matter these days. The software companies can't begin to keep up with the hackers, especially if the hacker is some government spook."

I knew he was probably right. I had just finished watching the season finale of *CSI Cyber*, a new TV show about computer and electronic crime. If even half of the stuff depicted on the show was true, the average citizen was a sitting duck for hackers to steal their identity and their passwords. Computers, phones, pretty much anything electronic was vulnerable. After watching the show, I was almost afraid to plug in my toaster.

I thanked them and headed home.

103

As I drove, I played over in my mind the day's events.

I couldn't figure how someone knew I had the manuscript on my computer, then it hit me. Frank Katz' computer was missing. Whoever injected him with the potassium chloride had undoubtedly taken it. All the perp had to do was look in Katz' 'sent' folder to discover he'd sent me a copy, and now, even that was gone. I had no way of knowing whether they could figure out I had downloaded it on a thumb drive before they infected my computer with the virus.

For Bob's sake, I hoped not.

I felt violated. Some asshole had been in my apartment and in my computer.

I was suddenly in a panic. I stopped by a branch of my bank, identified myself, and asked a matronly lady behind a desk to take a look at my checking account. I had no doubt the guy was probably sophisticated enough to totally wipe me out. Thankfully, our funds were intact and I breathed a sigh of relief. I told the lady I had been hacked and she told me how to contact tech support to change my password.

Back in the car, I thought about the intruder and wondered what else he might have done. I picked up the phone and called Kevin, my brother-in-law and partner in Walt Williams Investigations. He had been a P.I in Phoenix for thirty years and had all kinds of spy crap.

104

"Kevin, do you have one of those gizmos that can find electronic bugs which are hidden?"

"Does, Donald Trump have goofy hair?"

I took that as a 'yes' and had him meet me at the apartment.

I filled him in on what had transpired. He swept the entire apartment but found nothing.

"Any chance the thing can tell if my phone's been bugged?"

"Nope, that's something entirely different. There's no way to know exactly, but if I were you, I'd behave as though it was."

I thanked him, and as he was walking out the door, he turned, "Be careful, Bro. These guys play for keeps."

At that moment, I was frustrated and angry and I was really pissed that now I would have to pay all those bills by hand.

And to tell the truth, I was more than a little bit scared.

105

CHAPTER 11

True to his word, Ox had Judy call Maggie and the two of them cooked up an evening out for the four of us.

They had made reservations at Zio's Italian Kitchen which didn't exactly thrill me.

I'm not a big fan of ethnic foods except Mexican. I love tacos, burritos and margaritas, although food purists tell me the fare at Taco Bell has nothing in common with real Mexican food.

I'm more of a meat and potatoes kind of guy, nothing fancy, just the basics, as long as it contains one of the major food groups, gravy.

I see no reason to Kung Pao a poor chicken when you can fry it and have the resulting squeezings for a rich gravy.

Nevertheless, if Zio's Italian Kitchen made the girls happy, then I was willing to go along, because, as the old saying goes, 'if the girls aren't happy, nobody's happy.'

After we were seated, a server brought a loaf of warm bread, which I thought was a good start, but then he proceeded to pour some viscous liquid which looked like thirty weight motor oil into a dish of grass clippings.

After he had finished and proudly presented his concoction, I tapped him on the sleeve and asked if he might have a pat or two of butter in the kitchen.

That was definitely a faux pas. The poor fellow looked like I had beaten him with a stick.

"Just try it, Walt," Maggie urged.

Reluctantly, I tore off a hunk of bread, dipped it in the goo and took a bite. I was surprised. It was actually quite good. I said as much and the server brightened immediately. I had made his day.

While he was fetching our drinks, I checked out the menu. It was four pages double sided and there was not a single mention of gravy. I settled for a spicy chicken alfredo which turned out to be pretty good as well.

During the meal, I told my story from the beginning. Ox was my partner and for five years, we had shared everything. His wife, Judy, was also a cop and a very good one at that. I already mentioned hiding things from Maggie was not a good idea, so I figured good company over a good meal was as good a place as any to come clean.

To say Maggie was upset would be an understatement.

"Someone's been inside our apartment going through our things?"

"I'm afraid so. As far as I can tell he was just there to sabotage my computer."

"Walt, you promised you'd stay out of this. Now look what's happened."

"I'm trying my best to stay out --- really! That's why I handed the manuscript off to Thornhill."

Ox was still dubious. "Let me get this straight. You're saying there's this big government cover

107

up going on and the conspirators have murdered two people to keep them from talking."

I nodded.

"And yet, you don't actually have proof either of them was murdered."

I nodded again.

"Walt, if what you're saying is true, that means our government, the people sworn to protect us, are murdering citizens to cover up their crimes. Do you know how crazy that sounds?"

"I know how it sounds, but what about B-613? I know you and Judy watched *Scandal*."

In the TV show about life in Washington, the writers depicted a black ops group of professional assassins whose job was to eliminate any and all threats to the United States by any means necessary. The organization was so covert, it was even beyond the control of the president.

"B-613! Come on, Walt! That was a TV show for chrissakes! Surely you don't think ---?"

"Think what? That if these chemtrails were really part of our national defense system against nuclear warheads the government would think twice about eliminating any threats to that system? Remember Spock's words in *The Wrath of Khan*, 'Logic clearly dictates that the needs of the many outweigh the needs of the few.' How does the life of an eighty-two year old man and one pilot stack up against the possibility of a nuke landing in Times Square?"

He thought for a moment. "I see your point, but I'm still not seeing any evidence."

"What about the bogus people who stole Frank Katz' papers? What about my computer? That's evidence enough for me that there's something very sinister going on."

At that moment, the server arrived with our checks and our discussion was put on hold.

The ride home was quiet. We all seemed to be lost in our thoughts, at least I was.

Ox was driving and I noticed he was checking his rear view mirror more than usual.

Finally, he said, "I think you might be right."

"About what?"

"Everything. On the way to the restaurant, I noticed a black SUV with government plates behind us. I didn't think much about it, but here we are, two hours later and it's back again."

"You sure it's the same vehicle?"

"The plates are the same, so yes, we're being followed."

I thought for a moment "Keystone Kops?"

"Sure, why not," Judy replied.

At the next stoplight, Ox came to a screeching halt and Judy and I bailed out on opposite sides of the car and headed straight for the SUV. If there had been traffic behind them, we would have had them cold, but there wasn't. The moment our feet hit the pavement, the SUV's tires squealed as the driver shifted into reverse. After a quick u-turn, they sped off in the opposite direction.

When we were back in the car, I turned to Ox. "How's that for proof?"

The next morning I got a call from Jack Carson.

I hadn't heard from him since he went on his pilgrimage to interview Kristen Meghan, the Air Force bioengineer who had turned whistleblower.

"Walt, Jack here. I thought we should touch base. Anything new on your end?"

"Unfortunately, yes. Same place? Eleven-thirty?"

"I'll be there."

After being seated at Mel's, he asked, expectantly, "Well, what have you got?"

Lots of things had happened since our last visit, but I didn't share everything I knew. I told him that Frank Katz had died before he could get his manuscript published, but I left out the part about him sending me a copy. I knew if I told him the whole story, he would pressure Thornhill for a copy of the manuscript and that's what I was trying to avoid.

I told him about the four of us being followed, but I omitted the part about someone being in our apartment.

When I finished, he was deep in thought. Finally he spoke. "So Dale Fox dies in a car wreck on his way to meet me with evidence and we can't prove the car was tampered with, and Frank Katz dies of a heart attack just before publishing his manuscript and we can't prove it was anything but natural causes. Quite a coincidence, don't you think?"

"Sorry, I'm not much of a coincidence fan."

"Me either."

"So how was your visit with Kristen Meghan?"

"Dead end. She wouldn't even talk to me. Someone's put the fear of God in her."

"Can't say I blame her. If they really threatened to take away her child, that's pretty powerful stuff. So you struck out?"

"Quite the contrary. I had a very enlightening visit with a pathologist who has been studying the effects of the chemtrail fallout. Sorry, I can't tell you his name. He would only talk to me if I promised to only refer to him as an anonymous source."

"Sounds like someone's put the fear of God in him, too. So what did he have to say?"

"Remember that long laundry list of stuff which is being sprayed, the barium, aluminum, ethylene bromide, and so on?"

I nodded.

"Well, they've been spraying the stuff for over fifteen years now, and it's contaminated the air we breathe and the food we eat.

"Take aluminum, for example. It's a major component in these aerosols. Although it is our planet's most abundant metal, our body has no biological need for it. The Pesticide Action Network North America lists it as toxic to humans and yet, aluminum is commonly found in vaccines, deodorants, anti-perspirants, over-the-counter medications, soft drink and beer cans, baking powder, cake mixes, processed cheeses, and other food products and additives. So we digest this stuff, rub it on our skin and get injected with it and add to that all we're breathing from the chemtrails. Over the years, aluminum accumulates in the brain, tissues, and to a lesser amount the bones. It causes brain degeneration, dysfunction and damage due to the blockage and reduced blood flow and oxygen. The brain shrinks as brain cells die. This causes dementia. Symptoms include emotional outbursts, paranoia, forgetfulness and memory loss, speech incoherence, irritability, diminished alertness, changes in personality, and poor or bad judgment. All these are on the rise, and more than 4 million Americans are afflicted.

"Apparently the West Coast has been more heavily sprayed than other parts of the country. Remember me talking about the California drought being caused by the jet stream being diverted by HAARP?"

I nodded again.

"Well listen to this." He pulled a sheet of paper from a folder he had carried into the diner. "Soil and water samples are being tested at the top of Mt. Shasta, California, and in Siskiyou County, and the aluminum levels are high enough to kill a moose. The levels are off the charts with the highest reading so far at 4,610 times the maximum contaminate level for drinking water in the sunny state. A recent snow sample taken form Ski Bowl on Mt. Shasta showed 61 times the maximum contaminant level for aluminum in drinking water. Pretty scary stuff."

"No kidding!"

"Then there's the barium. It's been proven to adversely affect the heart. I suppose it's another coincidence heart disease is the leading cause of death in the United States. According to the CDC, it affects one out of every five Americans."

He looked at his notes again. "Then there's the rise in asthma and upper respiratory illnesses caused by breathing the particulate matter in the air. I could go on and on."

"No need. I get the picture. But if this is all true, how can the American people just stand idly by and let this continue? Why aren't people up in arms?"

"Good question, my friend. I could give you my answer, but I think the doctor I interviewed said it more eloquently that I ever could. Let me read you his words. *'It seems almost unbelievable that millions, maybe billions of people could look up at the sky and not notice the dramatic changes that have occurred from what it was in the mid-1990s. Then our sky was a gorgeous, deep blue. Clouds were a beautiful assortment of shapes. The sun was glorious. But people under 30 may not have a*

113

real sense of recollection about looking up every day and seeing this panoramic magnificence. Most of them are too busy texting or chatting on their cell phones. There are other issues to consider, as well. People are in their own comfort zones and denial is a very powerful human emotion. In the hustle and bustle of our everyday lives, how many people look up at the sky? It also takes huge courage, a very deep, internal willingness to examine politically motivated, corporate controlled media spin, and search for the real answers. Humans like their regular routines. To re-examine what we think we know, based on new evidence, takes a willingness to think outside the proverbial box --- to want to find out the truth not the pervasive Orwellian doublespeak that pervades our society. If everything in our daily routine belies what is truly going on, it requires fortitude to explore the unknown and to question the litany. Given these issues, since our collapsing society has so many different levels of deceit, the financial debacle, the lies and deceit of government, the emerging police state, the disasters which envelope our fragile environment, it becomes increasingly difficult just to maintain a daily routine and survive the economic depression and its daily fallout. Mainstream media does its supporting role and deceives us. Millions, like the proverbial lemmings, hasten to join the group demise.'"

When he finished reading, I remembered the Professor's words when I asked why people weren't screaming for answers, "Apathy, the curse of modern society. Why do only fifty percent of the voting population cast their votes in the presidential election? Frustration, as in you can't fight city hall. The government is just too big and powerful. Complacency, as in I'm doing all right, why rock the boat."

I sighed. "Well now I'm officially depressed. Thanks a lot."

"See!" he said. "That's exactly the reaction most people would have. *'The problem's just too big! I don't want to even think about it.'* Then they go on with their pitiful lives, talking and texting on their phones, taking their kids to soccer practice and trying to stretch their paychecks to the end of the month, not realizing or caring they are being poisoned with every breath they take."

"Holy crap, Jack! You sound like you're on some kind of holy mission."

"Maybe I am. The more I learn about this conspiracy, the more I want to share it with the world --- to shout it from the rooftops until someone listens."

"So what are you going to do?"

"I'm not waiting any longer. I've got a few more sources to check out, then I'm going to run a series of articles in the *Star*. People may not like what I'll have to say. They may even be scared by what I have to say, but they won't be able to ignore what I have to say."

"Are you sure your editor will go along with this? The paper's owners may not want to poke the bear with your stick."

"We'll see. If the *Star* won't run with it, I have other sources. I'll get it in print one way or the other."

I had to admire Carson's zeal. He was a man on a mission, and unlike me and probably most Americans, he wasn't afraid to speak out for what he believed.

I just hoped someone would listen.

CHAPTER 12

The next morning I was practicing my usual daily ritual of Wheaties, coffee and newspaper when a headline jumped out at me.

WikiLeaks: U.S. spied on 3 French presidents.

The article revealed the NSA had been eavesdropping on confidential conversations of French President Francois Hollande and other French officials.

Ever since my first conversation with Jack Carson about the chemtrails, the same question kept nagging at me: *If everything I had read about this covert government program was true and it had been going on for at least a decade and a half, why, in heaven's name aren't people screaming for an explanation?*

It's not like some kind of high-tech listening device which has been secretly planted. All one has to do is look up and see the trails streaking across the sky on a daily basis.

I totally understood the explanation of Jack's anonymous pathologist. The average guy on the street is just too wrapped up his daily struggles to give a damn, but not everyone is like that. Watchdogs like Arnie and Nick as well as experts in their field like the pathologist are constantly on the lookout for government shenanigans, so why haven't there been headlines exposing Operation Cloverleaf and the HAARP installation?

The other problem I had been struggling with was the magnitude of such a program. Again, if everything I had read thus far was true, such an undertaking would involve literally thousands of people. Chemical companies would have to manufacture and deliver the stuff which was being sprayed, ground crews would have to load the chemicals into the huge tanks in the bellies of the planes, and pilots and their flight crews would have to spread the stuff across our skies. Engineers of some kind would have to man the HAARP installation. Surely, over a fifteen year period, someone would come forward and say, *"This is what's going on and the world needs to know."*

Sure, there have been a few like Kristen Meghan, but her revelations were cut short by threats from her superiors. Dale Fox had told Carson any leaks about what he was doing would have dire consequences, and a week later he was dead. The young man I met at the hotel who served on Fox's flight crew feared for his life and all he was guilty of was not reporting what he knew to his superiors.

Given all these facts, there were really only two possibilities, the whole thing was just a hoax cooked up by conspiracy theorists with nothing better to do with their time, or the threat was real and the participants were afraid to speak out, intimidated by threats from the government.

118

The article in the morning paper gave me an idea.

If there was any organization not cowed by the federal government, it was WikiLeaks. They obviously had no qualms about exposing the NSA's snooping on French officials. The article even went on to say WikiLeaks had been associated with all the information leaked by Edward Snowden.

I fired up the new computer I had been forced to buy since the hard drive of my old one had been fried by an unknown intruder. Talk about intimidation.

I still hadn't got the hang of the new one. My old operating system was Windows XP. The new one was Windows 8, and I was totally lost. Jerry was more computer savvy than anyone else in the building, so I prevailed on him to give me a quick lesson. Naturally he had to add a bit of levity to my lesson, explaining that computers were like air conditioners. They worked fine until you started opening Windows.

I logged on to the WikiLeaks website. There were hundreds of articles on government activities, including one about a seaman on a United Kingdom submarine. The headline read, *Trident whistleblower: "nuclear disaster waiting to happen."*

Perfect! I thought. If they weren't afraid to run a story on a whistleblower warning of a nuclear disaster, surely there would be something from a chemtrail whistleblower.

I entered 'chemtrails' in their 'search' engine and only two obscure references popped up.

Sunday, December 20, 2009: Researcher Clifford Carnicorn, journalist William Thomas and Above Top Secret's Mark Allin will join George Knapp to try to get to the bottom of chemtrails. They'll address such questions as: Is the government spraying the population? What are the chemicals made out of? How are we being affected?

The second one read: *Weather modification efforts have been on the rise in countries like China and the United States. According to Thomas, the US Air Force is engaged in "weather warfare," using nanotech 'smart particles' to modify, steer, and target the direction of storms. In fact, emissions from Project HAARP were used during Hurricane Katrina to steer it away from facilities in Texas, he detailed.*

That was it. Nothing else. No in-depth expose from some guy making the chemical brew or a pilot who had sprayed tons of particulate into the atmosphere. Needless to say, I was disappointed, but at least there were references to chemtrails and HAARP.

While I was in a search mode, I did some more Internet digging and found references to GMACAG, Global March Against Chemtrails And Geoengineering.

What I discovered was this group had organized a march on April 25th of 2015 which was called World Chemtrail Awareness Day, and apparently there had been similar marches in preceding years.

According to the article, twenty-one countries had sponsored over a hundred events worldwide.

If this was such a big undertaking, I began to wonder why I had never heard of it. I read further and got a clue as to why.

We created a social media frenzy that exploded so fast, that Facebook intentionally started using their secret AI (Artificial Intelligence) auto script to block our posts, photos and event listings from circulating or being shared. This, along with a very long list of other broken features such as all forms of communication with fellow activists were magically not working at the most critical of times, just days before and leading right up until after the April 25, 2015 event.

Our GMACAG admin team even prepaid in full for advertising on Facebook to help with the promotions. After receiving payment in full, Facebook did not deliver on the agreed amount of advertising. Needless to say a legal law suit was immediately initiated against them.

We even had the weather network run propaganda smear campaigns of articles against us on every weather search page in most countries on the day of the April 25, 2015 GMACAG. Why would the weather network, and its shareholders, spend so much time, and add revenue space to what they called a theory by a small group of people?

If what they were saying was true, it smelled a lot like censorship.

Just for kicks, I logged onto the website of the *Kansas City Star* and entered *Chemtrail Awareness Day* into their search engine.

Since I read the paper every day, I knew they had run stories on every kind of march from police brutality to cruelty to animals. Anytime anyone got a group of people together to protest something or support something, the *Star* had a reporter there.

But there was not a single word on the worldwide event, Chemtrail Awareness Day.

As I was pondering all this, the phone rang.

A woman's voice came on the line. "Is this Walt Williams Investigations?"

"Yes, Ma'am," I replied. "This is Walt Williams. How may I help you?"

 "My name is Genevieve Shipley and I'm calling about my daughter, Louise. See's gone missing."

"Have you talked to the police?"

"Let me start from the beginning. Louise actually lives in St. Louis. When I discovered she was missing, I contacted the missing persons unit there. When I told them my daughter had disappeared in Kansas City, they suggested I call the police here, which I did. They took her information, but said since she had no history here, there wasn't much they could do. The officer

122

I talked to gave me your number. Can you help me?"

"How long has your daughter been in town?"

"She arrived the day before yesterday and checked into the Adams Mark Holiday Inn by the Sports Complex. We were supposed to meet at Denny's for breakfast the next morning, but she never showed. I've been trying to call her cell ever since but it goes straight to voice mail."

"Was she just in town for a family visit?"

"No, she said she had a business appointment. That's why she was staying at the hotel instead of with me."

"Do you know what the business appointment was about?"

"No, she said we'd talk about it at breakfast. Maybe it had something to do with the company she worked for."

"Which one is that?"

"Monsanto. Their world headquarters is in St. Louis --- on North Lindbergh Boulevard, I believe."

I had only been mildly interested in the case up to that point. Missing persons cases are notoriously difficult and rarely end well, but the moment she mentioned Monsanto, my ears perked up. The huge corporation had been mentioned frequently in the Internet searches I had done on chemtrails and geoengineering.

"Are you free to come to my office?"

"Certainly."

I gave her directions and asked her to bring a recent photo of her daughter if she had one.

As soon as I hung up from her, I dialed Kevin and told him to get his rear over here. We had a client.

An hour later, Genevieve Shipley had signed our retainer, paid our advance fee and given us a photo of Louise. I promised we'd keep her informed as our investigation proceeded.

When she was gone, I turned to Kevin. "Where do you want to start?"

"Her hotel room of course?"

"How do you propose we get in? Your picks are no good on those electronic locks."

"That's why I have this," he said, pulling an electronic gizmo out of a bag.

He never ceases to amaze me and that's why he's my partner.

On the way to the hotel, I filled Kevin in on what I had read about Monsanto.

The huge corporation was one of the primary beneficiaries of the chemtrail program. I read to him some of the stuff I printed off an organic food website.

Geo-engineering food companies such as Monsanto use the government's claim of slowing down global warming through chemtrails to justify the need for the GMO seeds. The problem with chemtrails is what goes up, must come down. These chemicals are seriously polluting our waterways and soil while seeping into crops and contaminating livestock, not to mention changing the weather patterns. Plants are especially sensitive to the soil degradation that occurs with chemtrail spraying, creating serious issues with our food supply.

Chemtrails are chemical or biological agents deliberately sprayed at high altitudes for purposes undisclosed to the general public in programs directed by various government officials. These sprays pollute the soil, water and air while compromising the health of humans, animals and plants. But wait – Monsanto has developed seeds that will weather the effect of the sprays, creating a tidy profit for the corporation while organics suffer.

Monsanto in cooperation with the government has designed genetically modified seeds which withstand the effects of chemtrails. The seeds are designed to survive extreme weather conditions, pollution, salt stress, heavy metals and chemtrails. Organic and natural crops will die from severe pollution and the chemtrails while Monsanto continues to profit. Further proof that the government and giant food corporations are controlling the food supply.

Take a look around your grocery store and realize that just about everything on the shelves contains something grown with Monsanto's patented gene splicing techniques and proprietary toxic pesticide concoctions. Then try to understand the scope of this complete takeover of our food production system.

Control the weather and you control food production. Get enough key players in the government, control American policy, control the weather through your connections or obtain inside information about that control, buy up all the major seed suppliers, and then you are in a position to force feed GMOs to America and every other nation that does business with America, your partner in one of the greatest crimes in history.

Kevin shook his head. "I had no idea it was so bad."

"Neither does your next door neighbor or the guy across the street. That's the way the players want it. As long as there's groceries on the shelf, the average Joe doesn't give a damn about what's in them or how they got that way."

We pulled into the parking lot of the Adams Mark Holiday Inn. Mrs. Shipley said her daughter was staying in room 518. We stopped at the front desk to make sure no one else was in the room. The last thing we wanted was to walk in on someone courtesy of Kevin's little electronic gizmo.

The clerk said the room was reserved for two more days, so we headed upstairs.

The hall was empty and I stood watch while Kevin hooked his machine to the door lock. A few minutes later, we were inside.

It was obvious Louise was not planning an extended stay. The one suitcase in the room was on the little folding thing and had not been unpacked.

"Nothing in the bathroom but some hairspray and the other gunk that women use," Kevin reported.

I spotted a piece of paper on the desk by the phone. It was a business card and the name on the front hit me like a brick. Louise Shipley had come to Kansas City to talk to Jack Carson.

CHAPTER 13

"Holy crap!" I said, picking up the card. "Dollars to donuts, Louise Shipley was a Monsanto whistleblower who had come to Kansas City to give Carson more dirt for his expose."

Then I noticed a thumb drive which had been hidden by the business card. "And I'd be willing to bet there's some juicy stuff on this thing," I said, holding up the drive.

"So what now?" Kevin asked.

"I think we'd better get Jack Carson over here. It's quite likely he's the reason she was in town and he may have some insight as to where she might be."

I started to dial Carson from my cell but then changed my mind and dialed from the hotel phone. I figured the less 'they' could tie me to Carson, the better.

"Jack Carson here."

"Jack, this is Walt. Does the name Louise Shipley mean anything to you?"

A long pause. "Maybe. Why do you ask?"

"Because she's missing and we're in her hotel room. I think you'd better get over here. Room 518, Adams Mark Holiday Inn at the Sports Complex. Oh yes, bring a lap top or IPad."

"Give me twenty minutes."

When Carson arrived, I held up his card. "Start talking."

129

He sighed, "It's a long story. A month or so ago, I was covering a series of home invasions and I took the time to interview several of the neighbors close to the homes that were hit. One of those interviews was with Genevieve Shipley. She was a nice lady, very cooperative and friendly. I ran the story and figured that was the end of it. Then one day, out of the blue, I got a call from her daughter, Louise. She said her mother had given her my number.

"Bottom line, she worked for Monsanto and was disturbed by some of the things she was seeing and figured the public should know what was going on. Naturally I was excited. According to everything I've found, Monsanto is right at the heart of this chemtrail thing, so I encouraged her to come to Kansas City and bring whatever information she had."

"That information is probably on this thumb drive," I said, holding up the device.

I could almost see Carson salivating. He reached for it, but I jerked it back.

"Not so fast. Louise is missing and we've been hired by her mother to find her. Have you had any contact with her since she arrived?"

"Yes and no. She called me and we made arrangements to meet for lunch, but she never showed. I've been trying to call, but everything goes straight to voice mail."

"Same as her mother," Kevin said "She was supposed to meet her for breakfast, but didn't show there either."

"So that's my story. Can we see what's on the thumb drive?"

I handed him the device, he booted up his lap top and plugged it into the USB port.

One of the first things that popped up was a photo of a map.

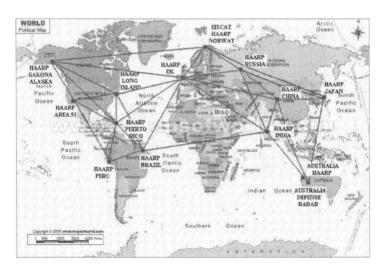

Carson let out a low whistle. "This is a map of HAARP installations all across the globe. Every continent is affected."

I remembered one of the passages I had read from the organic farmer's website. *Control the weather and you control food production. Get enough key players in the government, control*

131

American policy, control the weather through your connections or obtain inside information about that control, buy up all the major seed suppliers, and then you are in a position to force feed GMOs to America and every other nation that does business with America, your partner in one of the greatest crimes in history.

With the kind of global coverage pictured on the map, both the weather and food production could be influenced worldwide.

The next thing on the drive was an article about Monsanto partnering with the Weather Channel, supposedly so Monsanto could bundle more services to farmers who already buy their genetically modified seeds and herbicides.

I remembered the organizers of the Chemtrail Awareness Day wondering why the Weather Channel was running articles on their weather pages smearing the campaign and its organizers, and here was the answer. Monsanto and the Weather Channel were in bed together with the mutual goal of assuring the public the chemtrails were harmless because Monsanto had the resources and the products to save the world's food supply.

"Another nail in their coffin," Carson said, pocketing the thumb drive, "and it dovetails perfectly with the other information I've gathered."

He opened a file on his lap top.

"It gets worse. Do you remember when I gave you a partial list of all the things in our daily lives which contain aluminum: vaccines, deodorants, anti-perspirants, over-the-counter medications, soft drink and beer cans, baking powder, cake mixes, processed cheeses, and other food products and additives?"

I nodded.

"Then remember the data which confirms the metals such as mercury and aluminum aren't flushed from our bodies but collect in our brain cells and cause all kinds of neurological trauma such as dementia, Alzheimer's and even brain cancer?"

I nodded again.

"Well, guess what other chemical we're force fed, which facilitates the movement of soft metals across the blood/brain barrier to infiltrate our brain tissue. Fluoride! There have been over 34 human studies and 100 animal studies linking fluoride to brain damage, including lower IQ in children, and studies have shown fluoride toxicity can lead to a wide variety of health problems and yet over 67% of the nation's water supply is fluoridated. Today America is the sickest society on this planet ... made so in three short generations. Is it coincidence we are also the most Geo-engineered, vaccinated, GMOed, fluoridated and drugged society on the planet? America needs to wake up and smell the coffee before it's too late!"

"That's all well and good," Kevin, Mr. Practical, replied, "but we've got a missing girl to find. I say we flash her photo around downstairs and see if anyone saw her last night."

We started at the front desk. I showed the photo to the clerk.

"Oh, yes, Miss Shipley. Very pretty girl. The last time I remember seeing her was late yesterday afternoon. She was on her way to Casey's, our sports bar."

I thanked him and we headed into the bar. I showed the photo to the bartender.

"Yes, I remember her well. She sat at the bar, right over there," he said, pointing. "She ordered a cocktail and an appetizer. Her food had just arrived when her cell phone went off. After she read the message, she threw some bills on the counter and took off. Didn't take a bite or finish her drink."

Kevin tapped me on the shoulder and pointed to the surveillance camera in the corner of the bar.

I thanked the bartender and we went back to the reception desk.

"We need to see your surveillance footage from last evening," Kevin said.

The previously friendly clerk became defensive. "I can't just show you that. I don't even know you guys. Besides, I think you need a warrant."

"I'm sorry," Kevin replied. "Let's start over. My friend here and I are private investigators." He handed the clerk a card. "One of your guests, Miss

Shipley, is missing and we have reason to believe she's been abducted. We're trying to find her. Yes, technically we'd need a warrant if you weren't willing to share your footage with us, but it would mean involving the police and most likely, with all the commotion about someone being abducted from your hotel, a lot of your guests might check out and find some place safer. Is this what you really want?"

The clerk thought about it for a moment. "Okay, let's don't get people excited. Gina, come cover the desk, please."

He led us to the back office and started fumbling with dials. "What do you want to see?"

"Just Casey's during the time Miss Shipley was in the bar."

He fiddled some more and the images flashed across the screen. "There she is," Kevin said.

We watched, and the scene unfolded just as the bartender had said.

After she left the bar, Kevin said, "We'll need a copy of the footage. Now let's go to the camera which covers your parking lot."

The clerk shook his head. "Sorry, no can do. Some kids shot out the lens with a BB gun and we haven't got a replacement yet."

"Damn! Well, copy what you've got and we'll be out of your hair."

We thanked the clerk and gathered in the lobby.

"Time to get the cops involved," I said. "I'll make some calls."

135

I called Gino Ferelli at Missing Persons and we headed downtown.

We pulled into the parking lot just as Ox and his new partner, Amanda, were finishing their shift. I gave Ox a brief explanation why we were there and he asked if he could tag along.

After briefing Ferelli, he pulled the file. "Here it is. Genevieve Shipley called in and said her daughter was missing. Not much we could do at this point. Let's take a look at your surveillance footage."

I handed him the disk and he slipped it into the machine.

Just as Louise Shipley got up to leave the bar, Ox said, "Stop! Back up a few frames."

He looked closer at a man who had gotten up right after Louise and followed her out of the bar.

"I know that guy. That's Paulie Spiegel. We call him Paulie the Pervert. We arrested him about eight years ago. He was working at a gas station and had installed a camera in the women's bathroom. We arrested him in his apartment. He was watching some of his recorded videos and doing the hand jive, if you know what I mean."

"So you caught him red-handed?" Kevin quipped.

"Actually, if I remember correctly, I think he was right handed. I thought he was still in jail."

Ferelli punched a few keys on his computer. "Here he is. Paulie Spiegel, released three months

136

ago. I'll put out an APB and we'll bring him in for questioning.

Two hours later, Spiegel was in an interrogation room.

"What am I doin' here? I didn't do nothin'."

"We'll see about that," Ferelli said, turning on the video screen. "See the chick heading out of the bar? Well guess what? She's missing, and here's you, Paulie the Pervert, going out right behind her. I don't suppose you'd know anything about that?"

Paulie swallowed hard. "Yeah, I saw the chick. She was a hottie all right. I had just decided to make a move on her when her phone went off. She read some message and took off like a bat out of hell. I looked around and there weren't no one else I was interested in, so I went up to Harvey's Tavern up on Highway Forty. You can check with Gus, the bartender. I was there for three hours and still didn't score."

"My heart's broken," Ferelli replied. "I'm going to check with Gus and if your story doesn't hold up, you're gonna be in a world of hurt. Now get your ass out of here."

"Too bad," Ferelli said after Paulie was gone. "I thought we might have a good lead."

"Let's run her cell phone," I suggested. "I've got her number."

Ferelli led us to one of the technicians who entered her phone into his computer. After a few minutes, he said, "I've got a location for you. It's on Blue Ridge Cutoff, just a couple of blocks from the hotel."

We piled into the car and headed back toward the Sports Complex.

We parked on a side street and split up, searching both sides of Blue Ridge.

"Got it" Ox said, picking up the phone. "Whoever grabbed her must have tossed it. They knew we would be tracing it."

"Let's see what that important text was all about," Ox said, punching some keys. "Here it is. It says, 'Plans changed. We must talk tonight. Very important. Meet me in the hotel parking lot.' It's signed Jack Carson."

We all looked at Carson who was dumbfounded. "I --- I didn't send that message. I swear! I was at home all evening, working on my story. You can check the time stamp on my computer."

"We believe you, Jack. But someone knew the two of you we're getting together. Maybe we can find out who. Ox, call in the number that sent the text. Maybe we'll get lucky."

A few moments later, his phone rang. "Okay, thanks anyway." He turned to us, disappointed, "No luck. Burner phone."

"Jack, who knew about your meeting with Louise?" I asked.

"No one. I told absolutely no one, and I've been really careful about making calls. I even got a burner phone of my own just in case my cell and my land line were tapped."

"Where were you when you set up the appointment with Louise?"

"At home. Why?"

I thought about going home and finding someone had been in my apartment. I hadn't told Jack because then I'd have to explain about my screwed up computer and Frank Katz' manuscript.

"Just an idea. Kevin, do you still have the gizmo in the trunk that tracks bugs?"

"Does Monsanto have aluminium resistant seeds?"

I took that as a yes, and we headed to Jack's apartment.

We quietly followed Kevin as he swept the entire apartment. He paused, tapped his device, and checked the screen, then he put his finger to his lips and pointed to the smoke detector.

We huddled outside his apartment.

"There's a listening device in your smoke detector. Even though you used your burner to set up your meeting with Louise, someone overheard it, sent her the text and when she went to the parking lot --- well who knows what might have happened. Whatever it is, it's not good."

"So what should I do with the damn thing?" Jack asked.

"I'd leave it right where it is," Kevin replied. "If you get rid of it, whoever planted it will know you're on to them. Knowing they're listening just might come in handy before this thing is over. Just don't forget it's there."

"I couldn't possibly," he said. "This thing's getting darker every minute. Now it looks like three people are dead all because of this damned conspiracy."

He was right. The prospects of finding Louise Shipley alive were slim and none and it was my job to deliver the bad news to her mother.

CHAPTER 14

An article in the *Kansas City Star* drew my attention. The headline read, *Mass extinction is on the way, scientists believe.*

It went on to say that a study published by biologists in the journal, Science Advances, found that the Earth is losing mammal species at 20 to 100 times the rate of the past. *"We can confidently conclude that modern extinction rates are exceptionally high, and they are increasing, and they suggest a mass extinction under way. If the currently elevated extinction pace is allowed to continue, humans will soon, in as little as three human lifetimes, be deprived of many biodiversity benefits. We have the potential of initiating a mass extinction episode which has been unparalleled for 65 million years."*

Given what I had learned over the past few weeks, assuming it was true, it was no wonder things were dying off at a record pace. If some sinister cabal was indeed spraying aluminium, barium, ethylene dibromide, and God knows what else into our atmosphere, all of it had to eventually come back to good old earth and seep into the ground and water supply, thus affecting the planet's vegetation. The animals eat the poisoned plants, drink the polluted water, and Bingo, things start dying off.

The thing which was puzzling to me was the article never once mentioned geoengineering, chemtrails or weather manipulation. Why not? Was it because those things simply don't exist or because the influence of the cabal was so far reaching the scientists feared for their lives?

I was pondering these weighty issues when the phone rang.

It was Mary Murphy.

"Mr. Walt, is everything still a go for our picnic?"

"Oh crap!" I muttered under my breath. With all the chemtrail drama going on in my life, I had totally forgotten we had planned a picnic at the hotel to celebrate the Fourth of July.

In years past, we had gone to one of the massive celebrations with fireworks displays like the one at Riverside Park, but as we have gotten older, hunting for a place to park and fighting the huge crowds had become less appealing. We decided this year to all meet at the hotel and include the twenty residents there as a good will gesture.

Mary volunteered to be in charge of the food and assigned each of us dishes to share in pot luck fashion. Jerry was to be the emcee and plan the program.

"Uhhh, sure. As far as I know, everything's a go."

"Great! Make sure you and Willie get the folding tables over here early so I can get the food and drink tables set up."

Swell! I had totally forgotten I was half of the table committee. "I'm on it," I lied. "We'll be there bright and early."

I had to quickly shift gears from conspiracy mode to party mode.

One doesn't want to get on Mary Murphy's bad side.

Thankfully, the day was bright and the sun was shining.

As promised, Willie and I had the folding tables at the hotel at eight o'clock. We had just finished unloading when Ox showed up with a huge grill. He was in charge of hot dog, brat and hamburger production.

Kevin and his squeeze, Veronica, arrived with coolers filled with ice and all kinds of soft drinks. We had considered the possibility of this being a BYOB party, then nixed the idea given the fact that most of the tenants were either recovering alcoholics or problem drinkers.

Dad and Bernice had stayed up late baking cookies and other treats. I saw Dad slip a Tupperware container to Ox and I suspected that, in spite of our 'no booze' policy, it contained Jell-O shots, one of Dad's specialties and one of Ox's vices. I just hoped he wouldn't overindulge and set himself on fire at the grill.

Throughout the morning, people drifted in, bearing their favourite dishes to share with the group.

Mary had brewed ice tea and whipped together a cooler of lemonade. Once she caught Benny Finkle from room 12 trying to slip some vodka into the lemonade.

"You try that again, I'll hit you so hard it'll wake up your dentist!"

Benny gave her a big toothless grin. "Somebody done beat you to it."

Not to be outdone, Mary retorted, "Then I'll just punch you so hard you'll have to put toothpaste up your ass to brush the few teeth you have left!"

Apparently that convinced Benny and he stalked off.

Finally, just after twelve, everything was ready.

Jerry assembled everyone together and asked the Professor to offer a word of prayer.

As I looked at the group, I marvelled at the diversity. A retired university professor, a private eye, an ex-hooker, a real estate agent, a stand-up comic, twenty guys clinging to the bottom rung of the social ladder and two cops who would likely be arresting them under different circumstances. Where else but in America?

After the prayer, everyone lined up next to Ox's grill where he had been labouring diligently to have a stack of everyone's favourite meat ready to go.

144

With plates filled, people drifted off to find a shady spot to enjoy their meal. For many of the tenants, I suspect this was the best they had eaten in months.

When everyone had finished and tossed their paper plates into the trash can, Jerry called us to the porch. It was entertainment time.

I held my breath. You never knew what Jerry the Joker might come up with. He once celebrated Mary Murphy's birthday with plastic dog poop on her front step and a plastic ice cube with a bug in her glass of punch.

He asked us all to stand, then nodded to Mr. Beasley who opened the door to the hotel.

I was shocked as old man Feeney came through the door proudly carrying the American flag. A white sailor hat sat jauntily on his head. Then I remembered the old guy was a World War II veteran and had served on a destroyer in the South Pacific. I also knew he had few possessions in his tiny sleeping room, so the hat he wore must have been very special for him to have kept it for so many years. Around the hotel, Feeney was the butt of so many jokes because of his ability to stop up the plumbing, and his aromatic deposits were legend. I suddenly saw Mr. Feeney in a new light, knowing he was one of the many who had given years of his life in service to his country, and we were standing here today because he and the men of his generation had fought to preserve our way of life.

Jerry asked us to join in the Pledge of Allegiance, and when we were finished, he asked us to take a seat.

He solemnly picked up a sheet of paper and began to read.

Twas on this date in '76
Many years ago
That five brave men told old King George
That he would have to go.

And thus was born our country
Free from tyranny.
A new land of prosperity
From sea to shining sea.

In years to come there would be others
Who'd take our freedom away.
But none could conquer this mighty nation
That was born this special day.

We cannot take for granted
The freedom won that day.
For evil men throughout the world
Would take our gift away.

So we must join together
With those who've served before
To keep those who'd do us harm
Away from our country's door.

We love our lives of freedom
But the cost is never free.
It's bought with the blood of heroes
Who've died for you and me.

So on this very special day
Let's pledge ourselves anew,
To fight the fight for freedom
For the red, the white and the blue.

So that those who follow in our steps
May someday stop and see
That we have given all we have
To preserve our legacy.

We must stand fast together
So that we might save
Those precious things that make us
The land of the free and the home of the brave.

I saw old man Feeney wipe a tear from his eye and he wasn't alone.

Jerry reached back, punched a button on his boom box and the air was filled with Lee Greenwood's beautiful, *God Bless the USA*.

We all sat in silence listening to the stirring words.

And I'm proud to be an American
Where at least I know I'm free

And I won't forget the ones who died
Who gave that right to me

And I gladly stand up next to you
And defend her still today
Cause there ain't no doubt I love this land
God bless the USA

It was the perfect ending to a perfect day. Good friends, good food, good fellowship.

I was feeling happy and proud to be with these people and enjoy the blessings of life that we have, then I looked up into the blue sky and I saw six white trails crisscrossing from one end of the horizon to the other, and dispersing into a hazy cloud.

Suddenly my euphoria turned into apprehension and I remembered the words of Wil Durant, "A great civilization is not conquered from without until it has destroyed itself within."

I didn't understand what was happening, and it scared me to death.

148

CHAPTER 15

With the holiday over, it was time to get back to work.

Although there was little chance we would find Louise Shipley, I had promised her mother I would try.

We knew from the time stamp on the video, the time Louise had left the sports bar, but because the parking lot camera had been damaged, we had no idea what kind of vehicle might have carried her away.

The spot we had found her cell phone led us to believe the vehicle, whatever it was, had travelled north on Blue Ridge Cutoff. Geno Ferelli at Missing Persons pulled up traffic cam footage of Blue Ridge for a thirty minute period starting from the time she left the hotel. Ox and I ran the footage in slow motion, looking for any sign of Louise.

"There!" Ox said, pausing the video. "See that black SUV? It's just like the one that followed us from the restaurant the other night."

"Can you get a plate?" I asked.

Ox twisted dials and viewed the SUV from every angle available on the video, but the license plate never came into view.

"Nope, can't get it. Without a plate, it could just be a soccer mom taking her kid to practice."

We continued scrolling and I spotted something. "Hold it right there. The old Chevy. Isn't that Paulie?"

Ox isolated the Chevy and adjusted for a close-up view of the driver. The picture was grainy, but there was no doubt it was Paulie the Pervert.

"So he's heading north, right by where the cell phone was tossed." Ox said.

"But it fits with his alibi," I replied. "He said he was going to Harvey's Tavern on Highway 40, and that's north."

"Pretty convenient," Ox observed. "Who was his alibi again?"

"Gus the bartender," Ferelli chimed in. "I gave him a call and he confirmed that Paulie was there."

"What's Gus's last name?" Ox asked, punching some computer keys.

"Grinder," Ferelli replied. "Gus Grinder."

"Well, whadda you know," Ox said, staring at the screen. "Mr. Grinder is on the state's sex offender list. Got busted for taking photos up women's dresses with a toe camera. Whadda you bet that Gus and Paulie are peeping buddies?"

"If Paulie nabbed Louise, it wouldn't be a stretch to think he might have shared his good fortune in exchange for an alibi," I said. "I think we should pay Mr. Grinder a visit."

Harvey's was the typical sports bar with TV screens tuned to the latest sporting events.

A huge guy was polishing glasses behind the bar.

Ox moved toward the bar. "Are you Gus Grinder?"

"Who's askin'?"Grinder replied.

"I am," Ox said, holding up his badge.

"Yeah, that's me. Whadda you want?"

"Paulie Spiegel. You said he was in here a few nights ago. That true?"

"Yep, Paulie was here. Stayed about three hours, then took off."

"And you both were here the whole time?"

"That's what I said. If you don't believe me, ask Junior. He was here too." Gus motioned to a guy already blitzed, slumping in a corner booth. "Junior! Me and Paulie was both here the other night. Right?"

Junior opened one eye and nodded, "Yeah, right."

"See!" Gus said, arrogantly. "Told you so."

I was pretty sure if Gus had asked Junior if he had seen the pink ponies in the bar, he would have answered 'yes.'

"Mind if we take a look around?" Ox asked.

"Look all you want," Gus replied. "I got nothin' to hide."

We poked around the back room of the bar and found nothing to suggest Louise Shipley had ever been there.

I had no doubt she had been abducted, but by whom? Was it by paid assassins to keep her from sharing secrets about Monsanto's involvement in the chemtrail conspiracy, or Paulie the Pervert, the twisted peeping Tom?

We might never know for sure.

When I got home, I checked my email. I hadn't done it for a few days because I had been totally wrapped up in getting things together for our Fourth of July bash.

There was a multitude of the usual, people wanting to give me money and notifications I had won this or that lottery, but the one which caught my eye was from Jack Carson.

It read, *"Hi Walt. I really wanted to meet with you in person to discuss some new developments in our case, but I knew you were tied up with family things. Hope you have a great time. FYI, I have been doing some digging online and I found sixteen Facebook groups with over 63,532 members, dedicated to getting the word out about chemtrails and geoengineering. It gave me a big lift to know I was not in this alone and that others have seen the handwriting on the wall, or to be more specific, in the sky. Once I get my story done, I'll post it on those sites. Think about it. If each of those people share my story with only 50 friends, over 3 million people will finally see the truth. Let's get together after the holiday. Jack."*

I definitely wanted to tell him what we had found, or rather what we hadn't found about Louise Shipley's disappearance, so I called his cell. It went straight to voicemail. I tried his home number and got an answering machine. Then, as a last resort, I called the number of his new burner phone. There was no answer.

I looked up the number, called the *Kansas City Star* and asked to speak to Jack.

"I'm sorry, Mr. Carson isn't in." said a sweet young voice. She hesitated a moment. "Actually, he hasn't been in for two days. Have you tried his cell phone?"

I thanked her, hung up, and retrieved the last two days papers out of the recycle stack. I thumbed through both and discovered there were no bylines mentioning Jack's name. On a normal day, there would be at least a half dozen.

I put the papers away, climbed in my car and headed downtown to the *Star* building.

The city editor, Mike Gross, was a busy man, but took a few minutes to visit with me. I introduced myself and explained I had been working with Jack on a story, but couldn't reach him.

"Me either," he said, disgusted. "He's my #1 guy on the crime beat and he doesn't show for two days. I've had to send rookies out to get the stories. By the way, what story are you working on with him?"

"The one about chemtrails and geoengineering."

"Holy crap!" he exploded. "Not that conspiracy thing again! He's come to me several times wanting to run the thing and I've nixed it both times. He's just wasting his time pissing up a rope and he's gonna get some very important people's panties in a wad. I told him to drop it and concentrate on the real stories. There's plenty of them out there, for Christ's sake."

It was obvious Mr. Gross didn't share Jack's enthusiasm about the story. I saw no need to press him further. "Do you mind if I look at Jack's desk?"

"Help yourself," he said, pointing to an empty cubicle, "but you aren't going to find anything. Jack worked on the run. Did everything on his laptop and sent his stories in by email."

I thanked him and strolled over to the cubicle. He was right. There was nothing there but a few pens, paper clips, a candy bar wrapper and a box with two stale donuts.

My next call was to Kevin. We had both been to Jack's apartment when Kevin found the listening device in the smoke alarm. I asked him to meet me there with his lock picks.

We knocked quietly, but there was no answer.

Kevin went to work with his picks and soon had the door unlocked. Pressing his finger to his lips to remind me someone was listening, we entered the apartment.

Everything was pretty much like we had seen it before. I suspected Jack didn't spend much time there. There were no signs of a struggle and no notes left for someone to find. We searched everywhere, but found no laptop. If it wasn't at his office at the *Star* and it wasn't here, it had to be with him, wherever that was.

We slipped out, pulling the door closed behind us.

Back in my car, I was overcome with a feeling of dread.

First, it was Dale Fox who had died in a mysterious car accident, then Frank Katz of a suspicious heart attack. Most recently, Louise Shipley had vanished, and the one thing they all had in common was that they were going to tell the world about a covert government operation spewing poisons into our sky.

Now it was beginning to look like Jack Carson was missing too.

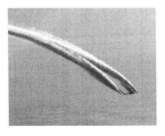

CHAPTER 16

My next stop was back to Missing Persons.

Geno Ferelli looked up in amazement. "Jesus, Walt. What now? You're running me ragged."

"You're Missing Persons aren't you?"

"Yeah, so what?"

"So I've got another missing person, Jack Carson, a reporter at the *Kansas City Star*."

Ferelli smiled. "I'm way ahead of you. Took the report this morning from his city editor, a Mike Gross. He's really pissed. Wants Carson back on the job ASAP. I've already turned it over to Homicide."

"Homicide? Is Jack Carson dead?"

"Not that I know of, but it's probably a good bet considering what he'd been into lately."

I assumed Ferelli was talking about the conspiracy theory and said as much.

"Don't know nothing about that," he replied. "Talk to Blaylock. He'll give you the scoop."

Derek Blaylock was one of the best detectives in the Homicide Division. As I headed to Homicide, I thought about my five years on the force. He and I had worked numerous cases together and developed a mutual respect.

"Walt, good to see you. What brings you to Homicide?"

"Jack Carson. Ferelli said he sent the case to you. What's going on?"

"Ahhh, yes, Jack Carson. Good reporter, but he couldn't just report the news. He always had to dig a little deeper and often found himself in deep doodoo."

"Any particular case come to mind?"

"Absolutely! Carmine Marchetti, which is why Ferelli sent the case over to me. He figured if Carson had bought the big one, Marchetti probably had something to do with it."

"How so?"

"Marchetti has always been on our radar. Everyone in town knows he's one of the Dons in the Kansas City mafia, but we've never been able to pin anything on him. On the surface, he's clean, but we know his legitimate businesses are just a front for his illegal operations. Some snitch supposedly gave Carson a tip which would connect Carmine to the protection racket in Northeast, and he jumped on it like a duck on a June bug. Bottom line, the snitch mysteriously disappeared and Carson came up empty, except, of course, for the lovely Calinda."

"And who might that be?"

"That's Carmine Marchetti's little girl. Carson met her during his investigation, and rumour has it the two of them hit it off pretty well, if you know what I mean. You can imagine Carmine wasn't exactly pleased when he found out the guy who was trying to write a story about his illegal operations was banging his daughter."

"So you think Marchetti is responsible for Carson's disappearance?"

"That's the theory, unless you have something better."

"I might," I replied. "How much time do you have?"

"As much time as you need, my friend. Let's hear it."

I started at the beginning and told him everything I knew about the story Jack was working on and the three previous deaths we believed were connected to the plot.

When I was finished, he leaned back in his chair. "Walt, have you ever heard of Occam's Razor?"

I nodded knowing what was coming next. "Yes, of course I have. It says when you have two competing theories that make exactly the same predictions, the simpler one is the better."

"Very good. Now look at the situation from my point of view. The prediction is Jack Carson is dead. On the one hand, we have a mafia don who's really pissed because the guy has tried to out him and now he's doing the nasty with his daughter. On the other hand, we have a theory there is a clandestine government conspiracy involving the Navy, Air Force, the CIA, the NSA and God knows how many other alphabet organizations, who are intent on spraying poison into our atmosphere to control the weather, prevent the Russians from pelting us with ICBM's and allowing Monsanto to take control of the world's food supply. Is that about right?"

He was right. My story sounded ridiculous compared to his.

I just nodded.

"Good. Glad you understand. Dollars to donuts, poor old Jack is at the bottom of the Missouri River wearing concrete sneakers. We'll probably never know for sure, and Carmine Marchetti, if he's really involved, will get away scot free. That's just the way it works sometimes. Sorry, Walt."

"Yeah, me too. Any idea where I can find Marchetti?"

"Jesus, Walt! Surely you're not going to ---?"

"I've got to know for sure. I owe it to Jack. So are you going to tell me where Marchetti hangs out or do I have to dig it up myself?"

Blaylock just shook his head. "Okay, but don't say I didn't warn you. Most days he has lunch at Antonelli's on Baltimore."

"Thanks, I owe you."

"Walt, be careful. Marchetti doesn't mess around. I'd hate like hell to be dragging the river for your body, too."

I assumed Antonelli's was typical of the Italian restaurants in Kansas City. I didn't have much to compare to because I wasn't a big fan of Italian food.

The maître d' met me at the door. "One for lunch today, Sir?"

"Actually, no. I was supposed to meet Carmine Marchetti for lunch," I lied. "Has he arrived yet?"

He looked at me suspiciously. "No, Mr. Marchetti hasn't reserved a table today. Possibly you have the wrong day on your calendar."

"That must be it," I replied. "Thanks for your time."

It was almost noon and I was getting the munchies, so I headed to Mel's for a chicken fried steak.

I had just parked and was headed to the diner when a black van pulled up beside me and two men who looked like movie extras from *On the Waterfront*, hopped out. They came up beside me and one whispered in my ear, "Mr. Marchetti would like a word with you."

"Uhh, I was just going to have a bite of lunch, can I --- ?"

He leaned in again and patted the bulge under his coat. "Mr. Marchetti wasn't asking."

"Got it," I replied.

He directed me to the van and I climbed inside.

The one driving turned and gave me a look. "Please buckle your seat belt."

I took his suggestion as a good sign. If I was on the way to the Missouri River, it probably wouldn't have mattered if I was buckled or not.

We headed downtown and pulled into an alley behind one of the multi-storied office buildings on Grand Avenue. The two goons escorted me to a freight elevator and punched the button for the penthouse.

As we headed to Marchetti's office, I was expecting to see a guy who looked like Marlon Brando's Vito Corleone character in the *Godfather* movie. Quite to the contrary, the man sitting behind the huge desk looked more like Frankie Laine, the old crooner from the 1950's.

I had expected a scowl, but he gave me a congenial smile and pointed to a chair directly in front of his desk. I sat, and the two goons, one on each side of me, took a step back.

"Mr. Williams, is it? So sorry I missed our luncheon date at Antonelli's. That's not like me."

Obviously news on the Italian grapevine travelled fast.

"About that," I stammered.

He held up his hand. "No need to make excuses. You wanted to talk to Carmine Marchetti, so here we are. Talk!"

I figured, *What the hell. I'm here. I might as well jump in with both feet.* "Thank you for seeing me. I'd like to talk to you about Jack Carson. He was a friend of mine and he seems to be missing. With all your connections, I just thought you might have some idea where he might be."

I wasn't sure what his response would be, but I was certainly unprepared for what followed. He looked at me for a moment like he couldn't believe what he was hearing, then burst into uncontrollable laughter.

When he finally composed himself, he gave me a sympathetic look.

"Very well said, Mr. Williams. Your friend is missing and you've come into my office to accuse me, in a very nice way, of course. What could possibly make you believe I had anything to do with his disappearance?"

I saw no reason to beat around the bush. "Rumor has it Carson was trying to get a story about your organization and in the course of his investigation, he met your daughter, Calinda, and there was, shall we say, a mutual attraction. I can't imagine you were pleased about such a turn of events."

This time his look was less amiable. "Mr. Williams, may I call you Walt?"

I nodded. What else could I do?

"Walt, this is not the roaring twenties and I'm not Al Capone in spite of what your friends at the precinct may have told you. I'm a businessman and I keep my nose clean. You probably already know there's not a single conviction on my record."

Obviously, Marchetti had done his homework and knew of my five years on the force. He undoubtedly knew way more about me than I knew about him.

162

I started to respond, but he raised his hand again.

"Walt, do you have children?"

I shook my head.

"Then it would be difficult for you to understand today's young people. They're so independent and they have so much technology at their fingertips. In answer to your question, yes, I knew about Carson and my daughter, and no, I was not pleased, but I was smart enough to know if I forbade her to see the man, it would only drive her away from me and into his arms. They would have found a way to communicate in spite of my wishes, so, as a father, I was hoping her infatuation would run its course. You came here wondering if I was responsible for your friend's disappearance, and here is my answer. I was not. My daughter is devastated and grieving horribly at this very moment. How do think she would feel about her father if she learned I had taken the life of the man she thought she loved?"

Marchetti was either a sincere father or the best liar I had ever seen, and given the circumstances, I wasn't about to question his veracity.

"Mr. Marchetti, thank you for seeing me and for your candor. Given what you've told me, I can now concentrate the search for my friend elsewhere."

"I'm so happy to hear that, Walt, and please give my regards to Detective Blaylock."

With that parting shot, he gestured to his henchmen who escorted me out of the room.

The black van returned me to Mel's parking lot, but somehow I no longer had the munchies. Being at the mercy of a mafia don can have an effect on one's appetite.

On the trip back to my car, I was thinking about what Marchetti had said, and if it was true, then I was back to the alternative theory of Jack's disappearance: a government assassin had taken him out so his story would never see the light of day. Blaylock could quote Occam's Razor all day long, but it didn't make the possibility less true.

As I headed back to my apartment, I racked my brain trying to figure out where to turn next. Jack Carson, along with the computer which held the story of the conspiracy, were both missing. With four people dead, all of whom were connected to the story, my better judgement told me to drop the case while I was still breathing, but I just couldn't let it go.

My cell phone buzzed, but knowing the accident statistics associated with talking or texting while driving, I ignored it until I pulled up in front of my building.

I reached for the phone and the message that flashed across the screen sent a chill up my spine. There was a picture of Maggie in front of the City Wide Realty office, and only two words, "STOP DIGGING!"

I was in shock, staring at my wife's photo, when the phone buzzed again. The next message had a picture of Maggie in front of our apartment, with the words, "BACK OFF!"

There was no question someone was sending me an ultimatum: forget about Jack Carson and forget about this stupid conspiracy theory or suffer the consequences. The consequences involved the person I loved more than anyone in the world. Whoever had sent the messages knew where Maggie worked and where she lived, and the implication was that I should drop the whole thing or Maggie, like the four others, could disappear at any time.

My breathing was labored and I had broken into a cold sweat. It took a good fifteen minutes for my heart to stop racing.

As soon as I had my emotions under control, I pulled back onto the street and headed to Arnie and Nick's place on Warwick.

I barged in and handed my phone to Nick. "I need to know who sent these. Can you help?"

He looked at the photos. "Jesus, Walt! This is serious stuff. Are you still working on the conspiracy thing?"

I nodded.

"Then if it's who I think it is, we're probably not going to find what you're looking for, but I'll try."

He examined my phone again, then punched some keys on his computer. A few minutes later, he looked up and shook his head. "Sorry, Walt. Burner phone. No way to trace it."

I had suspected that. "What if I hit 'reply' and sent a message back to them. Would they get it?"

"Maybe, maybe not. What usually happens is they'll use the phone once to deliver a message, then dump it so it can't be traced, but you can certainly try."

I grabbed the phone, hit 'reply' and typed the message, "I'm done! I'm out of it. Please don't hurt my wife."

I just hoped someone would see it.

On the way home, I had to consider two possibilities, neither of which gave me much comfort. If Carmine Marchetti was just feeding me a line of bullshit, and he had actually whacked Jack, the message could have come from him, or, it could have come from a black ops assassin who would have no problem adding one more body to keep the story buried.

Either way, I had already made up my mind I was through with the whole thing. I hadn't asked for this case and in fact, I had promised Maggie I wouldn't get involved, but then I did and she was the one whose life was in danger.

I vowed that as soon as she came home, I would tell her the whole story. Maybe we would even get out of town --- take a vacation --- until this whole ugly thing blew over.

That was my plan and I felt good about it.

CHAPTER 17

I was pleased with my plan and couldn't wait for Maggie to get home so we could plan our impromptu getaway. Maybe we would go to Branson and take in some shows, or even better, she had been bugging me about going on another cruise.

I wanted the evening to be perfect, so I chilled a bottle of Arbor Mist and whipped up my signature dish, tuna casserole. As soon as she got home, I would slip off her shoes, rub her feet and tell her how special she was to me.

I put some soft music on the CD player and waited for my sweetie to arrive.

Normally, unless she had a late showing, she was home by five, and like many old codgers our age, we had our supper between five-thirty and six. If she was going to be late, she would always call and let me know so I wouldn't worry.

At five-thirty, I was beginning to get a bit concerned and when I hadn't heard from her by six, I was in full blown worry mode.

I had the cell phone number of Doris, the receptionist at City Wide.

"Doris, Walt Williams here. I was just wondering if you'd seen Maggie this afternoon."

"Sure did. She got back from a showing about four-thirty and left right after that. Must have been just before five."

My next thought was she might have been in an accident, so I called dispatch at the precinct and asked about any accidents in Midtown between five and six. There had been none.

I was starting to panic, then it occurred to me, *Dumbass! Why don't you just call her cell phone?*

I dialled her number and it went straight to voice mail.

By this time it was six-thirty, and my worst fears were realized. Maggie wasn't coming home.

My mind began racing. I had sent the message saying I was out of the conspiracy business, but what if no one got it?

It was beginning to look like either Carmine Marchetti or some government assassin had taken Maggie and I had to consider both possibilities.

I thought about calling Ox, then I thought about calling Kevin, but the more I thought about it, it didn't make sense to get my best friend or my brother-in-law involved in something which might get both of them killed. I had gotten us into this mess, and it was up to me to get us out, or die trying.

Based on my visit earlier in the day, I figured my best bet was the government assassin.

Several times during our investigation, I had considered calling my half-brother, Mark Davenport. I didn't even know I had a half-brother until about five years ago when he arrived at our door unannounced. It turned out that he was the

169

product of one of my father's dalliances in his younger days as an over-the-road trucker.

Back then, he was working with the FBI, but had since transferred to Homeland Security. We had worked on several cases together including the All Star game in 2012 when terrorists attempted to blow the place up.

I had his cell phone as well, so I made the call.

Looking back, my greeting probably wasn't the most pleasant, but I was beside myself with worry.

"Mark, this is Walt Williams and some of your goons have kidnapped Maggie and I want to know what the hell's going on!"

"Walt! Calm down. What in the world are you talking about?"

I hadn't called him before because the story sounded so far-fetched. I didn't want him to think I was a complete idiot.

I figured at this point it didn't really matter, so I laid out the whole story.

"Then this afternoon, I get these texts with Maggie's photo telling me to back off, and now she's gone. Level with me, Mark. You're in Homeland Security, for chrissake! Is there really any truth to these chemtrail theories?"

"I understand why you're so upset. I would be too if it were my wife. Let me make some calls and I'll get right back to you."

I hung up and paced the floor waiting for his call. A half hour later, the phone rang.

"Walt, Mark here. The stuff you're talking about is way above my pay grade, but I pulled some strings and called in some favours. The bottom line is that no one in the U.S. government is involved in Maggie's disappearance."

"You're absolutely sure?"

"Absolutely. I have it from the highest authority."

I couldn't help wondering exactly how high that was, and then remembered the B-613 group from the TV show *Scandal*, which operated independently, without government oversight.

"Thanks, Mark. I appreciate your help."

"Listen, Walt. If Maggie doesn't turn up, don't hesitate to give me a call. I'll do anything I can to help on this end."

After hanging up, it occurred to me Mark had never answered my question as to whether there was any truth to the chemtrail theories.

If Mark was to be believed, it must be Carmine Marchetti.

I loaded my revolver, stuck it in my belt and headed to Antonelli's restaurant.

I wasn't really sure what I was going to do when I got there, but I had to do something. I had no doubt that Carmine could have me squashed like a bug before I could get to him, but I really didn't care. If I couldn't find Maggie and get her back, it really didn't matter what happened to me.

I parked and barged into the restaurant. The maître d' tried to slow me down, but I pushed him aside and looked around the dining room.

I spotted Marchetti at a table in the back, a pretty girl on each arm, and the two goons I'd seen earlier were keeping an eye on the other customers.

I charged toward the table and was nabbed immediately by the two guards.

Marchetti waved his hand and I was brought to his table.

"Walt! Twice in one day. To what do I owe this rather rude intrusion?"

For the second time that day, I saw no point in beating around the bush.

"My wife, Maggie, is missing and I think you have something to with it."

I saw the confused look on his face. He motioned to the guards who pulled out a chair and shoved me onto the seat.

"Under normal circumstances," he said, wiping his mouth with a napkin, "I would be upset by what you have just done, but you've peaked my curiosity. Tell me more about this ridiculous accusation."

I told him everything that had occurred since I left his office and reached for my phone to show him the photos. The goons had me pinned to the chair immediately.

"Uhhh, just the phone," I stammered.

Carmine nodded and the goons released their grip which I suspected would leave bruises.

I handed Carmine the phone and he studied both photos.

"I can see why you would be upset. If this were my Calinda, I would be too."

Then he leaned forward. "Walt, look into my eyes."

I leaned forward and we were staring at one another just a few feet apart.

"Walt, listen to me carefully. I swear on my mother's grave I did not send these messages and I do not have your wife. Do you believe me?"

There was no question that he was sincere.

I considered my answer very carefully.

"Yes, I believe you --- for now, but if I find out you've lied to me, I'll be back."

"I can live with that," he replied, leaning back in his chair, "because I'm telling you the truth."

One of the goons whacked me on the head. "What shall we do with him, boss?"

"Let him go, of course. I like him. He's got one big pair of cojones for an old guy. I have to admire someone who would barge in here and disrupt the dinner of Carmine Marchetti. A man who would risk his life for the woman he loves deserves our respect. Good luck, Walt. I hope you find your wife."

He waved again and I was jerked to my feet and escorted to the front of the restaurant and shoved out onto the sidewalk.

I sat quietly in my car thinking about what had transpired.

Both Carmine and Mark swore they had nothing to do with Maggie's disappearance. Either one of them was lying, or there was another player in the game I was not aware of.

I headed back to my empty apartment. I had to drive very slowly because it was hard to see through the tears which wouldn't stop falling.

CHAPTER 18

Needless to say, it was a rough night.

I knew I needed to sleep because I would need my strength and my wits about me for whatever might happen the next day, but it just didn't happen. I tossed and turned, then finally gave up and just paced the floor, reviewing over and over what had transpired up to that point. I knew I was missing something, but I had no idea what it was.

As the first light of the morning came peeking through the window, I put on a pot of coffee. My stomach was too upset for my bowl of Wheaties, but I needed the caffeine jolt to wake me up.

I climbed into the shower and stood there until the water turned cold, hoping some detail would pop into my mind which would possibly give me a clue about Maggie's abductor, but nothing came.

I was drying off when the phone rang.

"Mr. Williams, undoubtedly you have been concerned about your wife. Let me assure you she is safe and unharmed --- for the moment."

"Who is this?"

"My name is not important. What is important is you do exactly what I ask if you want to see your wife again."

"Well, it's important to me. I need to know who I'm dealing with."

"Very well then. My name is Angel Alvarez. Now, shall we get down to the business of getting your wife back to you?"

"I have no idea who you are. What could you possibly want from me?"

"The computer, of course."

My first assumption was he was looking for Jack Carson's computer which contained all his chemtrail research.

"Look, I don't have Carson's computer. I never did. What makes you think I have it?"

Silence on the other end. "Who is this Carson person? I don't know him and I certainly don't want his computer. I want the one that your wife has hidden away."

"You want Maggie's laptop? If you have her, you must also have her computer. She always has it with her."

"Not her computer, you fool. The one that was given to her. Let's stop playing games. You will get that computer to me or you will never see her again."

"No, please! I honestly have no idea what you're talking about. Let me talk to Maggie. Maybe she can help me figure out what you're looking for."

I heard a disgusted sigh. "Bring the woman."

A moment later, I heard him whisper, "I will be listening to every word, so be very careful what you say."

A shaky voice came on the line. "Walt, is that you?"

"Maggie! Are you okay? Have they hurt you?"

"I --- I'm okay for now, but I'm so frightened."

"I know you must be. We'll get through this. We always have. Who is this Alverez guy and what computer is he talking about?"

"Walt, this is all my fault. Remember my new listing --- Hector Ramirez' house which was seized by the DEU?"

"Yes, the Columbian drug guy. What about it?"

"If you'll recall, I had Consuela and her daughters clean the place from top to bottom. While they were cleaning, they found a secret compartment in one of the kitchen cabinets. There was a laptop computer inside. The drug guys just missed it. Anyway, Consuela brought it to me and I fully intended to turn it over to the DEU, but just got busy and it slipped my mind."

"So that's what he wants? Any idea what might be on the thing?"

"From what I've overheard, it has the record of all Ramirez' contacts, his suppliers and his dealers. Apparently Alvarez is planning to move into the Kansas City drug scene and needs that information."

"Enough!" Alvarez shouted in the background. "Tell him where you hid the computer."

"I --- I didn't hide it. Walt, the computer is in our office under my desk. It's in a brown paper bag --- just like it was when Consuela dropped it off."

I figured our conversation was about to be cut short. "Maggie, one more thing. Has Alvarez blindfolded you at all?"

177

"No, why do you ask?"

"Just curious. Maggie, I love you and I'll get you out of this --- somehow."

I heard Alvarez say, "Take her away!" Then he came back on the line. "So, Mr. Williams, now you know about the computer I want. It's very simple. I will exchange your wife for the computer. Bring the computer to a warehouse at --- ."

"Stop right there," I interrupted. "If you think I'm coming to a deserted warehouse, you're sadly mistaken. I'm more than willing to trade some stupid computer for my wife, but I need a show of good faith on your part. I need to know you're really going to let her go, so if you want this thing to go smoothly, I'll pick the spot for the exchange."

He thought for a moment. "Where do you suggest?"

"It has to be somewhere public --- somewhere with lots of people around --- the J.C. Nichols fountain on the Plaza. It's out in the open and there are plenty of witnesses. If you're on the up and up, we can make the exchange and no one will be the wiser."

"Very well," he conceded, "but remember this, those innocent bystanders you mentioned could easily turn into victims and I know you don't want that. If I even think I see a cop, you'll never see your wife again. Do you understand?"

"Perfectly."

"Good. I will expect you to arrive at noon, alone, no cops. Bring the computer, we'll make the exchange, and you and your lovely wife can have lunch on the Plaza."

"I'll be there."

When I hung up, I had a momentary sense of relief. At least I knew what I was dealing with. In a way, I was glad it was not a government assassin or a mafia hit man.

Then the feeling of relief turned into a feeling of dread. Alvarez had not been shy about telling me his name and he hadn't bothered to blindfold Maggie. I was sure Alvarez was not planning on leaving any witnesses who could identify him.

There was no way I was going to call the cops. I just couldn't risk it. I thought about calling Ox, but he's so huge, he doesn't exactly blend into the background, and if Alvarez had done his homework, he might even recognize him as an officer.

No, my best chance was with the old-timers I had used on many other occasions, Kevin, Willie and my dad. They were all old, but they were tough as nails and had been down this path before. I almost didn't call Mary Murphy, but I knew if she found out I had launched a rescue mission without her, she'd be pissed and not speak to me for a month. Actually, she was as formidable as any of the others on my team, having whacked an assassin with her baseball bat and shot an intruder who had threatened her with a switchblade.

179

I called Kevin first and asked him to meet at my apartment and bring a couple of extra guns from his stash. Then I called Dad and Willie. I told them to meet in my apartment as soon as I returned from the hotel with Mary in tow.

As I expected, she was almost giddy I had included her in our adventure. She grabbed her bat, took a couple of practice swings and declared she was ready for action.

When we were all gathered in my apartment, I shared what had transpired. Their first reaction was shock that Maggie had been abducted. Soon, the shock turned to anger and then to determination as we discussed how we were going to get Maggie safely away from the drug lord.

We decided Kevin would leave at eleven with Dad, Willie and Mary. That way they would already be at the fountain long before I arrived. They would fan out, blend into the crowd which was sure to be there, and have their weapons concealed, but ready if things went south.

When they were on their way, I checked under Maggie's desk, and sure enough, the laptop was there, wrapped in a brown paper bag.

I couldn't help but play the 'what if' game.

If the DEU guys had found the thing when they first searched --- if the Broker had given the listing to another agent --- if Maggie had turned it in the day Consuela brought it to our door --- none of this would have happened and Maggie would not be in the hands of a Columbian drug lord.

Then my mind switched gears and I did the same exercise with the chemtrail conspiracy. If Dale Fox hadn't contacted Jack Carson, both he and Jack would still be alive as well as Frank Katz and maybe even Louise Shipley. But he did and now they were all gone, and for what? We were no closer to learning the truth about the chemtrails than when we started.

It is said that justice is blind, and indeed Lady Justice is depicted with a blindfold covering her eyes. It almost seemed in this situation, her eyes were covered to prevent her from seeing the truth, and yet, in spite of the blindfold, somehow she keeps the scale balanced. With the deaths of these four good people, the scale had been tipped in favor of the bad guys, and I couldn't help but wonder how she would balance things out.

I looked at the clock. It was eleven-thirty. I just had time to get to the Plaza for my date with destiny.

It's sometimes strange where the mind can wander. On my way to the Nichols fountain, I thought about Gary Cooper in the 1952 western classic, *High Noon*. His destiny was to face a gang of thugs at the very hour I was to face Angel Alvarez. Cooper was all alone. My comfort was knowing my people were there and would have my back.

I parked and walked a block to J.C. Nichols Park.

181

As usual, there were people all around, enjoying the fountain and the bright sunny day. There was a young couple with a baby in a stroller, a mom and dad trying desperately to keep their toddler from splashing in the water, and an older couple walking hand-in-hand. In the grassy park next to the fountain, a dozen men were engaged in a game of flag football.

Interspersed with this group were my four friends. Dad and Willie were huddled over a checker board, Kevin had set up an easel and pretended to paint, while Mary was just laying back in a lawn chair, catching some rays.

I had just entered the park when two vans pulled up to the curb on J.C. Nichols Parkway. Three men got out of each van. I assumed the one in the lead was Angel Alvarez. He came directly to me while his men fanned out around the fountain.

He looked at the package I was carrying. "That better be my computer."

"It is," I replied, "and it's all yours as soon as I have Maggie."

He motioned to one of the vans and a seventh man opened the cargo door. I could see Maggie inside. She looked frightened, but otherwise unharmed.

"Your wife," Alvarez said, pointing. "Give me the computer, then you may go to the van and take her."

I shook my head, "It's not going to happen that way. You bring her to me and we'll make the exchange right here."

"I don't believe you're in a position to negotiate, Mr. Williams," he replied, patting the bulge under his coat. "There are a lot of nice people here and I know you don't want to see any of them hurt. Now get to the van!"

"No, I certainly don't, and I'm sure you don't want any of your people hurt as well."

I looked around, assuming my little posse would spring into action, but to my dismay, each and every one of them were being held by one or more of Alvarez' men.

"Sorry to disappoint you," he said with a sadistic smile. "I'm afraid your little ruse has failed. I knew you would try something and I've been following you all morning. Very clever idea, hiding your friends, but just not clever enough. Now give me that computer and we'll all just head to the vans and leave before some innocent bystander is injured."

Alvarez' men started pushing my friends toward the vans. Mary, of course, had no intention of going peacefully. She jerked her arm away from her captor.

"Your momma must be proud, you beatin' up on an old woman. If you didn't have your gun in my back, I'd show you a thing or two!"

The man just scoffed and gave her another shove.

I knew once we were in the vans, we were all dead meat. Alvarez had no intention of letting us go. I wasn't about to give him the satisfaction of a complete victory.

"Sure," I replied, "we'll go quietly, but there's something I have to do first."

"And what might that be?"

"This!" I replied, tossing the computer into the center of the fountain.

I saw the look of shock on his face and figured he would probably gun me down right where I stood, but after a moment, he composed himself.

"I had planned to make your demise as swift and painless as possible, but now you will die a slow and agonizing death as will your wife and friends. Now get to the van or I'll gun you all down right here, along with these innocent people."

Just as we all started moving away from the fountain, the twelve men playing flag football suddenly sprinted to our little group, and in an instant, Alvarez' men were disarmed and their hands bound with plastic ties.

I heard a familiar voice. "I'm afraid, Señor Alvarez, that you're not going anywhere but to jail."

The voice was that of Carmine Marchetti.

"Good day, Walt. I hope I'm not intruding."

I breathed a sigh of relief. "Quite the contrary. But how --- ?"

"Let's just say you got my attention. I'm rather proud to say I have a reputation as a man not to be trifled with, and yet two times yesterday, you got in my face, first accusing me of murdering Jack Carson and then abducting your wife. Few men would have the audacity to do such a thing."

"Sorry about that. I was at my wit's end and audacity was about all I had left."

"It served you well. After your last visit, I just had to know what you would do next, so just like Mr. Alvarez, I had you followed. Fortunately, my men spotted his men following you. "

"You knew Alvarez?"

"I knew Hector Ruiz. He had come into my city with his Columbian drugs. I must say I was pleased when your Drug Enforcement Unit put him out of business. We had heard Alvarez was following in his footsteps. I simply put two and two together and surmised that your wife must have found something of value in her listing on Sunset Drive and that Alvarez had abducted her to get it back."

"You don't miss much, do you?"

"In my business, it's important to be well informed."

He looked at the bag in the fountain. "I suppose that's what he was looking for."

I nodded. "Laptop. It had all of Ramirez' contacts, both his suppliers and his dealers."

He looked at it wistfully. "Too bad it's ruined. With that information, you could have put an end to the Columbian's drug activity once and for all. It would have been good for my business"

"Probably still could," I replied. "I might have copied the files on a thumb drive before I left the house."

His face broke into a big smile and he clapped me on the back. "Well done! I knew I liked you."

About that time, Maggie rushed to my side and threw her arms around me.

"Ahhh, yes," Marchetti said, taking Maggie's hand. "You must be Mrs. Williams, a very special lady indeed to have your man risk his life to save you."

He bowed and planted a kiss on her hand.

Carmine was one suave Italian.

I gently removed Maggie's hand. "Yes, she is special, and I want to thank you for what you did today. I owe you."

"Nonsense! We both simply did what was right. Maybe someday the shoe will be on the other foot and I'll need the assistance of a fine private investigator. Who knows?"

It wasn't exactly comforting, knowing I was in debt to a mafia godfather, but at that moment, I was just happy we were all alive and in one piece. If Carmine wanted to call in my chit later on, I'd deal with it then.

I heard sirens in the distance.

"I took the liberty of calling your Detective Blaylock," Marchetti said. "If you have things under control here, I think it might be best if my men and I were not here when he arrives. Too many questions, if you know what I mean."

"I think we can handle it from here," I replied, extending my hand. "Thanks again."

"You're most welcome," he replied, giving my hand a firm shake.

After he was gone, Mary came huffing and puffing to where Alvarez was standing. She got right in his face. "This is for abducting my Maggie, you scumbag."

Without another word, she planted her foot squarely between his legs.

He crumpled to the ground moaning and gasping for air.

Mary turned to the other seven and sneered, "Anyone else want a piece of this action?"

They all cowered in fear.

Just before Blaylock arrived, I pulled Alvarez into an upright position.

"I need you to answer a question for me."

"Screw you," he retorted.

"No problem. Mary, come over here. I think you need to have another conversation with Mr. Alvarez."

"No! Keep that crazy woman away from me! What do you want to know?"

I showed him the photos of Maggie with the warnings to back off.

"Did you send these? Tell me the truth or I'll let Mary have her way with you."

He looked at the photos. "I've never seen those before. I swear!"

I almost wished that he had.

Someone had sent them, and I still had no clue as to who it might be.

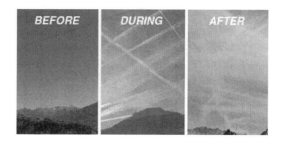

EPILOGUE

I was out of the conspiracy business.

I had promised Maggie I would be, and I intended to keep that promise.

Someone out there had told me to back off with a not-so-veiled threat that if I didn't, something would happen to the one person I love more than anything else in this world. I had almost lost her to Angel Alvarez and I wasn't about to tempt fate again.

Even though I knew it was the right thing to do, I still felt a pang of guilt.

If the chemtrail thing was truly a conspiracy, the world needed to know about it.

A quote from Albert Einstein kept running through my mind. "The world will not be destroyed by those who do evil, but by those who stand by and do nothing."

I didn't want to be one of the ones standing by, but I couldn't help thinking about what happened to four others who tried to warn the world they are being poisoned.

One moment my rational self would say the conspiracy theory was nothing but a hoax, then I would look at the evidence again and have second thoughts.

Maybe the brake line on Dale Fox's car was worn and simply ruptured at an inopportune moment, preventing him from delivering hard evidence to Jack Carson.

Then again, maybe not.

Maybe Frank Katz' poor old heart just gave out on him before he could publish his revealing thesis. His doctor said he had a bum ticker.

Then again, maybe not.

Maybe poor Louise Shipley was done in by Paulie the Pervert and Gus Grinder just before she was to reveal Monsanto's connection to the chemtrails.

Then again, maybe not.

Maybe Jack Carson really is at the bottom of the Missouri River, compliments of mafia boss, Carmine Marchetti. After all, he was banging the godfather's daughter.

Then again, maybe not.

But even if we say all those maybes are true, there are still a lot of unanswered questions.

Who were the men who claimed they were from the university and took all of Frank Katz' papers, including his thesis?

Who broke into my home and planted a virus on my computer to destroy the copy of the thesis that Katz had emailed to me?

Who broke into Jack Carson's home and planted a listening device in his smoke detector?

Who were the men in the SUV who followed us home from the restaurant?

And most important to me, who sent the pictures of my wife, threatening her life?

Since I was out of the conspiracy business, I would probably never know the answers to these questions and they would haunt me for the rest of my life.

My one hope was the manuscript I had given to author Robert Thornhill.

He called one day, saying he was almost finished with the first draft of the novel he titled, *Lady Justice and the Conspiracy.*

I liked the name. I've always been a fan of Lady Justice, because somehow, she always finds a way, often quite an unorthodox way, to balance the scales of justice.

Maybe this work of fiction might be the very thing that would reach the masses with the truth. Few of us would take the time to read a boring scientific treatise on the subject or take seriously the rantings of a guy wearing a tin foil hat, but who doesn't like to lose themselves in a good mystery novel?

Thornhill claimed to have a broad fan base, and a marketing program that would put the novel in over forty thousand homes.

Surely there would be those who would glean the kernels of truth from the pages of his book.

He promised to send me an autographed copy when it was in print.

For me, the events of the past few weeks have changed my life forever.

Every now and then the verse from Lee Greenwood's song plays in my mind.

I'm proud to be an American, where at least I know I'm free.

When I think of what I've seen and heard, I wonder if that freedom is just an illusion. Are we really free when deadly toxins are forced upon us in the air we breathe, the water we drink, the food we eat, and the vaccines that are injected into our bodies?

Every time I step outside I will look to the heavens for the white streaks that crisscross the sky from one horizon to the other, and wonder what witches potion is being sprayed that day.

Then I'll say to myself that the fluffy trails are simply water vapor frozen into ice crystals.

Then again, maybe not!

Conspiracy?

Check out these references, as Walt did and decide for yourself.

The Air Force Document titled, *Dominating the Weather 2025*
http://csat.au.af.mil/2025/volume3/vol3ch15.pdf

Operation Indigo Skyfold
http://stateofthenation2012.com/?p=10890

Project Cloverleaf
http://www.disclose.tv/forum/project-cloverleaf-chemtrails-and-their-purpose-t72795.html

HAARP
http://www.globalresearch.ca/haarp-secret-weapon-used-for-weather-modification-electromagnetic-warfare/20407

Pinal Air Park, Marana, Arizona
http://stopnortherncaliforniachemtrails.blogspot.com/2014/12/pinal-county-airpark.html

ECHELON
https://en.wikipedia.org/wiki/ECHELON

Monsanto
http://www.geoengineeringwatch.org/chemtrails-killing-organic-crops-monsantos-gmo-seeds-thrive/

http://weatherpeace.blogspot.com/2013/08/connecting-dots-monsanto-and-weather.html

http://www.triplepundit.com/2013/11/monsantos-climate-corp-predicting-weather-controlling-food-prices/

Aerial Vaccines
http://preventdisease.com/news/12/011712_Look-Up-The-New-Age-of-Inoculation-is%20Aerial-Vaccines-and-Nano-Delivery-Systems.shtml

http://www.geoengineeringwatch.org/vaccinations-from-the-sky/

Dr. Len Horowitz – Conspiracy Theorist
http://www.bariumblues.com/flu_conspiracy.htm

Kristen Meghan – Air Force Whistleblower
http://www.trueactivist.com/military-scientist-whistleblower-says-yes-we-are-being-sprayed/

Geoengineering
http://www.geoengineeringwatch.org/

http://www.collective-evolution.com/2014/04/18/nasa-admits-to-chemtrails-as-they-propose-spraying-stratospheric-aerosols-into-earths-atmosphere/

Chemicals
http://www.globalresearch.ca/chemtrails-the-consequences-of-toxic-metals-and-chemical-aerosols-on-human-health/19047

Fluoride
http://fluoridealert.org/articles/50-reasons/

http://www.globalhealingcenter.com/health-hazards-to-know-about/where-the-yellow-went

Videos

https://www.youtube.com/watch?v=c34U0Pwz4_c

https://www.youtube.com/watch?t=23&v=lZaD-H_j3pU

https://www.youtube.com/watch?v=mcZaJEMsSwM

Global Conspiracy?

What Do You Think?

Naarden, Holland

Canberra, Australia

196

Liverpool, England

Wales

Berlin, Germany

Amsterdam, Netherlands

198

ABOUT THE AUTHOR

Award-winning author, Robert Thornhill, began writing at the age of sixty-six and in five short years has penned twenty-one novels in the Lady Justice mystery/comedy series, the seven volume Rainbow Road series of chapter books for children, a cookbook and a mini-autobiography.

Lady Justice and the Sting, Lady Justice and Dr. Death, Lady Justice and the Vigilante, Lady Justice and the Candidate, Lady Justice and the Book Club Murders, Lady Justice and the Cruise Ship Murders, Lady Justice and the Vet and Lady Justice and the Pharaoh's Curse won the Pinnacle Award for the best new mystery novels of Fall 2011, Winter 2012, Summer 2012, Fall 2012, Spring of 2013, Summer 2014 and Fall 2014 from the National Association of Book Entrepreneurs.

Many of Walt's adventures in the Lady Justice series are anecdotal and based on Robert's real life.

Although Robert holds a master's in psychology, he has never taken a course in writing and has never learned to type. All 32 of his published books were typed with one finger and a thumb!

His wit and insight come from his varied occupations, including thirty-three years as a real estate broker. He lives with his wife, Peg, in Independence, Missouri.

Visit him on the Web at: http://BooksByBob.com

LADY JUSTICE TAKES A C.R.A.P.
City Retiree Action Patrol
Third Edition

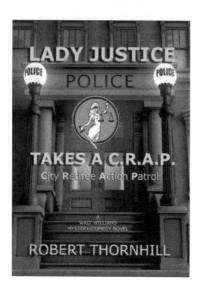

This is where it all began.

See how sixty-five year old Walt Williams became a cop and started the City Retiree Action Patrol.

Meet Maggie, Willie, Mary and the Professor, Walt's sidekicks in all of the Lady Justice novels.

Laugh out loud as Walt and his band of Senior Scrappers capture the Realtor Rapist and take down the Russian Mob.

http://amzn.to/16lfjnY

LADY JUSTICE AND THE LOST TAPES

Second Edition

When corrupt politicians, the Italian mob and a dirty cop collude to take over a Northeast neighborhood, Walt is recruited for the most bizarre undercover assignments of his new career.

When conventional police work fails to solve the case, once again his band of scrappy seniors come to the rescue.

In the process, the amazing discovery of a previously unknown session by a deceased rock 'n' roll idol stuns the music industry. What should be a joyous occasion soon turns dark as lives are threatened.

All of your favorite characters, along with two lovable additions are back to help Walt in his quest for justice.

Their adventures and misadventures are sure to keep you captivated – and splitting your sides!

amzn.to/1twzOfq

LADY JUSTICE GETS LEI'D

Second Edition

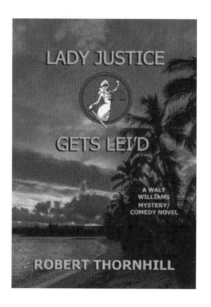

In *Lady Justice Gets Lei'd*, Walt and Maggie plan a romantic honeymoon on the beautiful Hawaiian Islands, but ancient artifacts discovered in a cave in a dormant volcano and a surprising revelation about Maggie's past, lead our lovers into the hands of Hawaiian zealots.

http://amzn.to/15P6bLg

LADY JUSTICE
AND THE
AVENGING ANGELS

Second Edition

Lady Justice has unwittingly entered a religious war. Who better to fight for her than Walt Williams?

The Avenging Angels believe that it's their job to rain fire and brimstone on Kansas City, their Sodom and Gomorrah.

In this compelling addition to the Lady Justice series, Robert Thornhill brings back all the characters readers have come to love for more hilarity and higher stakes.

You'll laugh and be on the edge of your seat until the big finish.

Don't miss *Lady Justice and the Avenging Angels!*

http://amzn.to/1xXrYdY

LADY JUSTICE AND THE STING

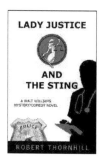

BEST NEW MYSTERY NOVEL ---WINTER 2012

National Association of Book Entrepreneurs

In *Lady Justice and the Sting*, a holistic physician is murdered and Walt becomes entangled in the high-powered world of pharmaceutical giants and corrupt politicians.

Maggie, Ox Willie, Mary and all your favorite characters are back to help Walt bring the criminals to justice in the most unorthodox ways.

A dead-serious mystery with hilarious twists!

http://amzn.to/1gS4JMA

LADY JUSTICE AND DR. DEATH

BEST NEW MYSTERY NOVEL --- FALL 2011

National Association of Book Entrepreneurs

In *Lady Justice and Dr. Death*, a series of terminally ill patients are found dead under circumstances that point to a new Dr. Death practicing euthanasia in the Kansas City area.

Walt and his entourage of scrappy seniors are dragged into the 'right-to-die-with-dignity' controversy.

The mystery provides a light-hearted look at this explosive topic and death in general.

You may see end-of-life issues in a whole new light after reading *Lady Justice and Dr. Death*!

http://amzn.to/H20Erx

LADY JUSTICE AND THE VIGILANTE

BEST NEW MYSTERY NOVEL – SUMMER 2012

National Association of Book Entrepreneurs

A vigilante is stalking the streets of Kansas City administering his own brand of justice when the justice system fails.

Criminals are being executed right under the noses of the police department.

A new recruit to the City Retiree Action Patrol steps up to help Walt and Ox bring an end to his reign of terror.

But not everyone wants the vigilante stopped. His bold reprisals against the criminal element have inspired the average citizen to take up arms and defend themselves.

As the body count mounts, public opinion is split.

Is it justice or is it murder?

A moral dilemma that will leave you laughing and weeping!

http://amzn.to/1d3FLK6

LADY JUSTICE AND THE WATCHERS

Suzanne Collins wrote *The Hunger Games*, Aldous Huxley wrote *Brave New World* and George Orwell wrote *1984*.

All three novels were about dystopian societies of the future.

In *Lady Justice and the Watchers*, Walt sees the world we live in today through the eyes of a group who call themselves 'The Watchers.'

Oscar Levant said that there's a fine line between genius and insanity.

After reading *Lady Justice and the Watchers*, you may realize as Walt did that there's also a fine line separating the life of freedom that we enjoy today and the totalitarian society envisioned in these classic novels.

Quietly and without fanfare, powerful interests have instituted policies that have eroded our privacy, health and individual freedoms.

Is the dystopian society still a thing of the distant future or is it with us now disguised as a wolf in sheep's clothing?

http://amzn.to/15P5LEE

LADY JUSTICE AND THE CANDIDATE

BEST NEW MYSTERY NOVEL – FALL 2012

National Association of Book Entrepreneurs

Will American politics always be dominated by the two major political parties or are voters longing for an Independent candidate to challenge the establishment?

Everyone thought that the slate of candidates for the presidential election had been set until Benjamin Franklin Foster came on the scene capturing the hearts of American voters with his message of change and reform.

Powerful interests intent on preserving the status quo with their bought-and-paid-for politicians were determined to take Ben Foster out of the race.

The Secret Service comes up with a quirky plan to protect the Candidate and strike a blow for Lady Justice.

Join Walt on the campaign trail for an adventure full of surprises, mystery, intrigue and laughs!

http://amzn.to/19f3XVZ

LADY JUSTICE AND THE
BOOK CLUB MURDERS

Best New Mystery Novel – Spring 2013

Members of the Midtown Book Club are found murdered.

It is just the beginning of a series of deaths that lead Walt and Ox into the twisted world of a serial killer.

In the late 1960's, the Zodiac Killer claimed to have killed 37 people and was never caught --- the perfect crime.

Oscar Roach, dreamed of being the next serial killer to commit the perfect crime.

He left a calling card with each of his victims --- a mystery novel, resting in their blood-soaked hands.

The media dubbed him 'The Librarian.'

Walt and the Kansas City Police are baffled by the cunning of this vicious killer and fear that he has indeed committed the perfect crime.

Or did he?

Walt and his wacky senior cohorts prove, once again, that life goes on in spite of the carnage around them.

The perfect blend of murder, mayhem and merriment.

http://amzn.to/1aWGg3K

209

LADY JUSTICE
AND THE
CRUISE SHIP MURDERS

Best New Mystery Novel – Summer 2013

National Association of Book   Entrepreneurs

Ox and Judy are off to Alaska on a honeymoon cruise and invite Walt and Maggie to tag along.

Their peaceful plans are soon shipwrecked by the murder of two fellow passengers.

The murders appear to be linked to a century-old legend involving a cache of gold stolen from a prospector and buried by two thieves.

Their seven-day cruise is spent hunting for the gold and eluding the modern day thieves intent on possessing it at any cost.

Another nail-biting mystery that will have you on the edge of your seat one minute and laughing out loud the next.

http://amzn.to/16VjURw

LADY JUSTICE
AND THE
CLASS REUNION

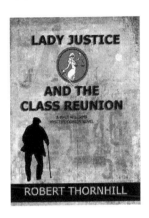

For most people, a 50th class reunion is a time to party and renew old acquaintances, but Walt Williams isn't an ordinary guy --- he's a cop, and trouble seems to follow him everywhere he goes.

The Mexican drug cartel is recruiting young Latino girls as drug mules and the Kansas City Police have hit a brick wall until Walt is given a lead by an old classmate.

Even then, it takes three unlikely heroes from the Whispering Hills Retirement Village to help Walt and Ox end the cartel's reign of terror.

Join Walt in a class reunion filled with mystery, intrigue, jealousy and a belly-full of laughs!

http://amzn.to/17S9YE0

LADY JUSTICE AND THE ASSASSIN

Two radical groups have joined together for a common purpose --- to kill the President of the United States, and they're looking for the perfect person to do the job.

Not a cold-blooded killer or a vicious assassin, but a model citizen, far removed from the watchful eyes of Homeland Security.

When the president comes to Kansas City, the unlikely trio of Walt, Willie and Louie the Lip find themselves knee-deep in the planned assassination.

Join our heroes for another suspenseful mystery and lots of laughs!

http://amzn.to/1bDdrKJ

LADY JUSTICE AND THE LOTTERY

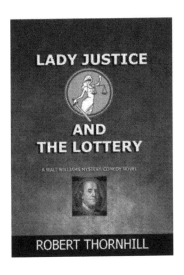

Two septuagenarians win the lottery's biggest prize, dragging Walt and Ox into the most bizarre cases of their career.

The two 'oldies' are determined to use their new found wealth to re-create the past but instead propel Walt into the future where he must use drones and Star Trek phasers to balance the scales of justice.

When an extortion plot turns into kidnapping, Walt must boldly go where no cop has gone before to save himself and the millionaire.

Come along for another hilarious ride with the world's oldest and most lovable cop!

http://amzn.to/1exhji6

LADY JUSTICE AND THE VET

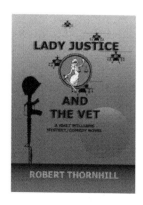

Ben Singleton, a Marine veteran, had returned from a tour of duty in Afghanistan and was having difficulty adjusting to civilian life.

Fate, coincidence, or something else thrust him right into the heart of some of Walt and Ox's most difficult cases.

Our heroes find themselves knee-deep in trouble as they go undercover in a nursing home to smoke out practitioners of Medicaid fraud, meanwhile, Islamic terrorists with ties to the Taliban are plotting to attack one of Kansas City's most cherished institutions.

Join Walt and his band of senior sidekicks on another emotional roller coaster ride that will have you shedding tears of laughter one minute and sorrow the next.

http://amzn.to/17GyE3n

LADY JUSTICE
AND THE
ORGAN TRADERS

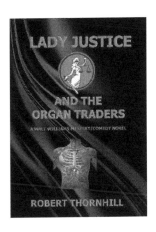

A badly burned body with a fresh incision and a missing kidney leads Walt into the clandestine world of an organ trader ring that has set up shop in Kansas City.

Walt is determined to bring to justice the bootleggers, who purchase body parts from the disadvantaged and sell them to people with means, until a relative from Maggie's past turns up needing a kidney to survive.

Once again, Walt discovers that very little in his world is black and white.

LADY JUSTICE
AND THE
PHARAOH'S CURSE

An artifact is stolen from the King Tut exhibit, setting in motion a string of bizarre murders that baffle the Kansas City Police Department.

A local author simultaneously releases his novel, *The Curse of the Pharaohs*, attributing the deaths to an ancient prophesy, 'Death shall come on swift wings to him who disturbs the peace of the King.'

Are the deaths the result of an ancient curse or modern day mayhem?

Follow the clues with Walt and decide for yourself!

http://amzn.to/1yHlnGE

LADY JUSTICE
IN THE EYE OF THE STORM

With the death of a young black man, Walt and Ox are dragged into the eye of a storm as Kansas City erupts in violence and demonstrations.

Fearing for their lives, Captain Short sends them on assignment to Cabo San Lucas where they find themselves in the eye of a very different and even more dangerous storm --- Hurricane Odile.

Surviving these ordeals pushes both men beyond the limits of anything they have experienced, and leaves Walt facing one of the most important decisions of his life.

amzn.to/1w6CthZ

LADY JUSTICE
ON THE DARK SIDE

After five years on the police force, a bullet in the kiester from a vengeful gangbanger convinces Walt that it's time to turn in his badge.

Walt realizes once again that retirement just isn't his cup of tea, and with a little urging from his brother-in-law, decides to become a private investigator.

For five years he had served the Lady Justice wearing a white robe and a blindfold and followed the rules, but he soon discovered that the P.I. business was leading him across the line into the dark side and a completely different set of rules.

When Walt comes face to face with the Lady Justice on the dark side, dressed in a tight skirt, fishnet stockings and high heels, he is faced with decisions that will change the course of his life.

amzn.to/1LFIDyS

LADY JUSTICE
AND THE BROKEN HEARTS

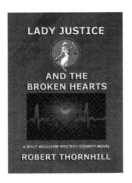

Walt goes under the knife for a heart operation and while in the hospital, stumbles upon a series of mysterious deaths that are certainly not from natural causes.

He solves that mystery only to discover that people on the transplant waiting list are suddenly dying as well.

Then, information about a terrorist plot is found on a heart attack victim who has been rushed to the ICU.

Throughout it all, Walt discovers that there are many ways that a person may die of a broken heart.

http://amzn.to/1I1xTIW

WOLVES IN SHEEP'S CLOTHING

In August of 2011, I completed the fifth novel in the *Lady Justice* mystery/comedy series, *Lady Justice and the Sting*.

As I always do, I sent copies of the completed manuscript to several friends and acquaintances for their feedback and comments before sending the manuscript to the publisher.

Since the plot involved a holistic physician, I sent a copy to Dr. Edward Pearson in Florida.

Dr. Pearson loved the premise of the book and the style of writing, particularly as it related to alternative healthcare, natural products and Walt's transformation into a healthier lifestyle.

In subsequent conversations, Dr. Pearson shared that he had been looking for a book that he could share with his patients, colleagues and peers that would spread his message in a format that would capture their imagination and their hearts.

The Sting was very close to what he had been looking for and he made the suggestion that maybe we could work together to produce just the right book.

As I reflected on this idea, I realized that Walt's skirmishes with pharmaceutical companies, corrupt politicians, doctors, nurses, hospitals, bodily afflictions and a healthier lifestyle were not confined to just *The Sting*, but were scattered throughout all six of the *Lady Justice* mystery/comedy novels.

Using *The Sting* as the basis of the new book, I went through the manuscripts of the other five *Lady Justice* novels and pulled out chapters and vignettes that fleshed out the story of Walt's medical adventures.

Thus, *Wolves in Sheep's Clothing* was born.

Dr. Pearson is currently using *Wolves* in conjunction with his New Medicine Foundation to help spread the word about healthcare alternatives.

New Medicine Foundation
Dr. Edward W. Pearson, MD, ABIHM
http://newmedicinefoundation.com

RAINBOW ROAD
CHAPTER BOOKS FOR CHILDREN
AGES 5 – 10

Super Secrets of Rainbow Road

Super Powers of Rainbow Road

Hawaiian Rainbows

Patriotic Rainbows

Sports Heroes of Rainbow Road

Ghosts and Goblins of Rainbow Road

Christmas Crooks of Rainbow Road

For more information,
Go to http://BooksByBob.com